DAYCARE MOM TO WIFE

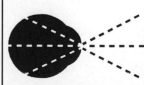

This Large Print Book carries the
Seal of Approval of N.A.V.H.

DAYCARE MOM TO WIFE

JENNIE ADAMS

THORNDIKE PRESS

A part of Gale, Cengage Learning

GALE
CENGAGE Learning

Detroit • New York • San Francisco • New Haven, Conn • Waterville, Maine • London

GALE
CENGAGE Learning™

LIBRARY OF CONGRESS CATALOGING-IN-PUBLICATION DATA

Adams, Jennie.
    Daycare mom to wife / by Jennie Adams. — Large print ed.
      p. cm. — (Thorndike Press large print gentle romance)
    ISBN-13: 978-1-4104-4169-0 (hardcover)
    ISBN-10: 1-4104-4169-5 (hardcover)
    1. Single fathers—Fiction. 2. Infants—Fiction. 3. Nannies—Fiction. 4. Large type books. I. Title.
    PR3619.4.A327D38 2011
    823'.92—dc23   2011031373

Published in 2011 by arrangement with Harlequin Books S.A.

Printed in the United States of America
1 2 3 4 5 6 7 15 14 13 12 11

Dear Reader,
What a thrill it is to be part of the Babies and Brides themed month.

And what fun I had taking the lovely Jess Baker and her baby daughter, Ella, and throwing them into the middle of a single-dad family.

There is such richness and fulfilment to be found in "stretching out our borders" to embrace and love those who cross our paths, be that a baby, a bride, a wonderful man, a ready-made family or all of the above. When we fall in love at the same time, there can be challenges aplenty, but oh, they can be worth it!

When Jess and Dan meet, they both believe they are better off by themselves. But fate has another plan for them, one that involves five children, a baby and, eventually, wedding bells and a wonderful (if noisy, busy, sometimes scary and definitely challenging) happy ever after.

I hope you enjoy my plucky independent Jess and her down-to-earth Dan as they figure out their journey and eventually take

their leap of faith into all that life has for
them.

With love and hugs from Australia,
Jennie

For my babies and for my rent-a-kids. I am so blessed. My life is the richer for each and every one of you.

CHAPTER ONE

'After we visit the ducks, there's got to be more knocking on doors for you and me, Ella. I know you'd probably rather be crawling around the furniture at home, but this is how it has to be for this morning.' Jessica Baker spoke the words to her daughter as she pushed the baby stroller over a rough patch of grass and let her glance rove around Randurra's memorial park.

Not that Ella could understand, but it made Jess feel better to speak out loud, to remind herself she did have a plan.

Ahead on the wide knoll beside the duck pond children were playing. A tall, dark-haired man watched them from beneath a gum tree. He was talking on his mobile phone.

Life went on whether people were trying not to shake in their boots or not. Jess didn't want to be someone who shook in her boots. She might wobble just a little here and there, but Jess was a single mother supporting her daughter. She couldn't afford to shake.

Any more than you can afford that enormous back bill of overdue rates and interest payable on the house.

Ten years' worth that Jess hadn't known existed, thanks to Ella's con artist father and the agreement he had made when he purchased Jess's small cottage, in exchange for Jess signing herself and Ella out of his life for ever.

Jess stiffened her spine and took one hand off the stroller to smooth it over her gold sleeveless top and down over the splash-dyed orange and black skirt. 'We'll be right, Ella. We'll sort this out somehow.'

In the stroller, Jess's daughter made a crowing noise. 'Du! Du!'

'Yes, indeed. We're going to see the ducks. You've earned that for being such a good girl this morning.'

Ella's vocabulary had a lot of 'Du' words in it, but in this case Jess was quite certain that her one-year-old knew exactly what she was talking about. Ella wanted to see the ducks before Jess finished her door-knocking and went home.

Jess's gaze moved ahead to the children. Two teenaged boys wrestled each other on the grassy bank. A studious-looking girl of around ten had hold of a smaller girl's hand and was warning her not to go too close to the water. A third little girl had plonked down on the grass to pick blades of it. As a potential offering for the ducks?

'Let's go add our bread crusts to the offering, Ella.' Jess wasn't afraid of bunches of children. She looked after five regularly to bring in income. She'd had four more but that family had left Randurra at the start of December.

Jess had been trying since then to get more work. She was a qualified daycare mum. This morning when her financial situation had shifted from 'already uncomfortable' to 'downright scary' with the arrival of that notice about the overdue rates and interest, Jess had taken her efforts directly to the people of Randurra. She'd knocked on a lot of doors. She'd offered to do anything. It didn't have to be childcare so long as she could keep Ella with her.

Breathe, Jessica.

Jess and Ella were drawing closer to the duck pond area. The man had his gaze fixed on the children in that way that said 'father'. Were they tourists going somewhere for the long school summer holidays and had stopped here for a breather?

11

Jess's heart did a funny flip as the man turned his head and she caught a good look at his face. He appeared to be around thirty-six or thirty-seven. He was tall, with tanned skin and a firm jaw and thick, wavy, dark brown hair that just touched the collar of his white polo shirt. He had jeans on. Tan lace-ups on his feet. It was a warm day, but not killer hot as it had been in the few days straight after Christmas. Jess wanted to see his eyes.

No, she didn't.

All those children meant he must be married.

Jess wasn't looking for a man anyway. After the fiasco of Peter, Jess couldn't trust in that sort of relationship any more.

'No. You're a key client and the financials have been under my care for a long time. I want to be the one to do this work.' The man's voice was low, deep and utterly calm as he spoke into the phone.

But his posture had stiffened and as Jess drew closer she caught a glimpse of very genuine stress as his gaze roved over those five children before he asked for a little time to 'get things in place', and abruptly ended the call. In that one moment, he looked as Jess had felt this morning when she read the notice saying the house would be sold up if she didn't pay all the costs in thirty days or less.

The man looked out of his depth.

As though he was asking how he could fix this.

What had happened? Jess wondered.

She watched the man suck it all inside, paste on his previous expression and just stand there. But inside, his mind was racing, searching for those answers. Jess knew because Jess had done this.

'Can I help you somehow?' She spoke the words before she could stop herself, and made a gesture with her hand. The row of wooden bangles on her arm clanked. 'It's just that you were on the phone and you looked . . .'

She didn't want to say he'd looked panicked. Truly he looked far too strong to give in to outright panic.

Strong and appealing and manly.

All entirely irrelevant, Jessica Baker, and you're just as strong.

Occasional very justified bouts of the wobbles notwithstanding!

Jess cleared her throat. 'I'm a local. Did you need directions, or information about services or anything?' She might sound like an animated travel brochure now, but that was better than noticing the man as, well, *as a man.*

'Uh, hello. Thanks . . .' Deep hazel eyes fringed with thick black lashes searched her face, and then dropped to Ella where she sat in the stroller crowing in delight to see so many children playing near her.

He had beautiful eyes. Eyes that showed his age and maturity, and that made Jess's breath catch.

Did his eyes hold a hint of consciousness within them, too? Jess was twenty-two, a lot younger. She'd never noticed a man this age quite so much. She didn't really understand her reaction and . . . she wondered if she was correctly reading his.

He seemed to give himself a mental shake before he responded. 'That's kind of you. We just moved here so I don't have a good grip on everything about Randurra yet.' He extended his hand. 'Dan Frazier.'

Well, that was all about business so maybe Jess *had* imagined the other.

'Jess Baker. Jessica, really, but I prefer Jess. I moved here about fourteen months ago.' Just in time to settle into the cottage before she made the short trip to the local hospital to give birth to Ella. 'So I know pretty much everything there is to know about the town.'

She tried not to stutter over the words, because the touch of Dan's fingers closing around hers gave her the strangest feeling of . . . comfort. And made her too aware of him. She took a deep breath and lifted her hand to check that the green band in her hair was straight, its enormous bow sitting firmly. Did Dan Frazier think she was an airhead because of that bow? Jess wasn't. The clothing and accessories were part of keeping her head up, of showing her determination in her own way.

Life had thrown a major curve ball today, but she hadn't let that stomp her. She'd put on her bright clothes and had marched to the town council building. She'd done her best to calmly and rationally discuss the situation with that nasty man who'd delivered the overdue notice, Lang Fielder. It had been to no avail today but she wouldn't stop at one go!

And then she'd knocked on half the doors in Randurra, looking for work. Jess still had the other half to knock on. She wasn't stomped yet.

'Da-a-ad.' A girlish voice came their way. 'Rob and Luke are going to fall into the water.'

'Are not.' A voice halfway to his father's deepness replied. 'We're just playing, Daisy.'

'Well, stop it. Don't you know there'll be approximately fifty thousand different kinds

15

of germs in that pond?' The girl called Daisy pushed a pair of glasses up her nose in a knowing and disapproving way.

Jess stifled a smile.

'Maybe you can point me in the direction of childcare facilities in Randurra, if anywhere exists here that caters for a family group with this age range.' Dan's hand reached down to touch the silky hair of the youngest child, who'd come running to wrap her arms around his legs.

He met Jess's gaze again as he pushed his mobile phone into the breast pocket of his polo shirt. 'I thought I'd have time to check out various childminding possibilities. I didn't expect to need this kind of care more than rarely, anyway, but it appears the Frazier family's two-days-old sea change just ran into a typhoon.'

Randurra wasn't on the coast, of course. It was inland from Sydney. Apparently that phone call had produced a metaphoric typhoon that meant Dan Frazier needed urgent childcare for the whole family.

Could Jess be so lucky? 'I may be able to help you. What exactly do you need?'

'Oh, I don't need much.' He gave one short bark of laughter. 'Just the equivalent of Mary Poppins to fly down with her umbrella and volunteer to mind all my children while I travel to and from Sydney for the next few weeks, and for me to know they'll all be safe with her when she's a total stranger and I don't like leaving them with anyone.'

He frowned again. 'My sister used to cover the times when I had to work away from home, but I weaned right off needing that, and she's got her own life to focus on now.'

There was no mother in the picture? Was Dan a widower? Jess's mind boggled at the thought of him raising five children by himself. Peter hadn't even been prepared to be a part-time father to Ella from long distance.

Some other part of Jess that really should know better also insisted on pointing out Dan's single status.

A single status and almost twice your age, Jess!

'So you moved here, you didn't need childminding, and now something's exploded?' Better to ask about that. 'Is it to do with your work? Did it make a very big splat as it hit the wall?'

'That's a creative analogy.' He didn't smile, exactly, but the creases at the corners of his eyes did.

Dan went on. 'One of my clients needs to go through a potential change of ownership

17

audit, and the prospective buyers want it done fast. I'm the company's accountant so I have to be on hand to help answer all the number-crunching questions, and supply the necessary information and explanations to go with it. This is a large key client for me, and they want this change of ownership. It's going to benefit the company tremendously and I need to hold on to their business, so I can't afford not to help.'

His gaze shifted over her hair and returned to her eyes. 'I moved the children here to get us all out of Sydney, into a decent-sized home that we could own ourselves. I thought I'd have all of January without having to think about work at all.'

'You can't blame yourself for the unforeseen.' She touched his arm briefly.

She only meant to express understanding and perhaps a little of the compassion that Mary Poppins might have extended when she finished folding her umbrella.

But it didn't end up feeling like only a touch. Dan's skin was warm and . . . manly. A tingle shot up Jess's arm.

Beneath her fingers, Dan's muscles locked as though he, too, had perhaps been startled by the contact. For a moment their gazes meshed and a consciousness passed between them.

Jess hadn't expected to feel such a strong connection. They had only just met. He was heaps older. She wasn't going there again with any man after the way Peter had hurt her. She withdrew her hand.

Over by the pond, one young Frazier after another fell still and silent.

Four sets of hazel eyes locked onto Jess, and baby Ella, and their father.

One whisper drifted to Jess on the summer breeze. 'Daddy's talking to a *girl*.'

Another. 'They're practically holding hands. He hasn't been near a girl since Mummy died.'

'Shut up, Rob. Shut up, Mary.' This came from the eldest boy. 'Whoever that is, Dad's not interested like that!' The boy sent a sharp stare Jess's way before he turned away, shoulders tensed beneath his T-shirt.

Jess felt put in her place, a woman far younger than this man and, indeed, why would Dan be interested?

You don't want *him to be interested, Jess.*

And perhaps the boy hadn't meant to sound so aggressive? He was probably used to dealing with all his younger siblings and occasionally got frustrated with them . . .

Had Dan heard those whispers? How long ago had he lost his wife? Had Jess misread his reaction when she touched him?

Had he wished she *hadn't* touched him? Or reacted . . . as Jess had reacted to him?

'Sorry about them. They're a little excitable thanks to the move.' Dan's neck had reddened slightly.

So he had heard. At least some of it.

'No need to apologise.' She ignored the neck. Well, other than the tanned, muscled appeal of it. Jess had to ignore that, too. Because widowed didn't necessarily mean emotionally available, even if the red was a result of consciousness of her, not simply embarrassment thanks to his children.

Not that it mattered to Jess one way or another, of course. Jess was very much *not* ready to jump into that particular pond again herself. She really needed this work and couldn't afford to let anything so foolish as a sudden attraction mess it up, if she could actually get Dan Frazier to employ her.

She *had* knocked on half Randurra's doors. She'd got nowhere. She had tried not to worry that she might get nowhere with the other half. Folks all seemed to have their childcare and other needs sorted out.

And perhaps Jess and Dan Frazier *could* help each other. 'Dan, I realise we've only just met and I haven't flown down with an umbrella like Mary Poppins. Actually, my brolly's black with pink polka dots and half the spokes are bent out of shape because I got it jammed under the seat of the car one day.' Jess drew a breath.

'But I'm a qualified, practising daycare mum.' An underemployed one at the moment. 'I care primarily for younger children but I am trained to take school-aged children as well.' If those opportunities came along. Jess spared a thought for the surly expression of Dan Frazier's eldest a moment ago, but if there were any problems she could win him over, surely? 'There aren't any official "Before and After School" style of care facilities in Randurra for school-aged children.'

Jess didn't want to tell Dan any more. She wanted to stick with 'I think I can help you', be Mary Poppins for him, Jess style, and they'd both benefit.

Instead, she drew a breath. 'There are two women older than me with grown-up children of their own who've recently become unemployed because the meatworks outside of town downsized. They haven't been in childcare professionally before but they're great women. I'm looking for more work, but I saw from the noticeboard at the supermarket that they're both looking for work in that line, too, or a combination of that and housekeeping. So you've got some choice and I too would be happy to help out with housekeeping duties.'

'If you have training with children . . . Are you saying you're available?' Dan's gaze seemed to travel over each feature on her face.

When his gaze rested briefly on her mouth, her lips wanted to soften. Instead, she forced a bright smile. He was probably just thinking she was way too young for the job. 'What exactly is it that you need for your children, Dan?'

He seemed to drag his gaze from her mouth and his brows drew together.

Dan Frazier *was* a little attracted to her. And from that look, he didn't want to be.

Well, there you were. Jess didn't want that, either. They were on the same page, even if she didn't know *his* reasons for that fact.

He was heaps older than her, a widower and father of five and a potential employer. Did he even have to have any other reasons? *Jess* didn't need any other reasons to stifle her consciousness of him out of existence than those she'd just listed. And that was *without* mentioning Peter.

'I need someone to watch the children up to five days a week at my home for somewhere between the next three to six weeks or so. It would help a lot if that person could also take care of laundry and meals and some other basic housekeeping.' Dan drew a breath. 'This work I have to do is going to mean long hours at home for a while for me. As well there'll be trips to Sydney maybe up to three days a week until it's sorted.' His hand rose to rub briefly at his breastbone before he dropped it back to his side.

In three to six weeks, working five days a week for Dan Frazier, Jess could really earn some money to help towards those repayment instalments. The money wouldn't pay the debt off but it might convince Councillor Fielder that Jess could *get* the money to keep making decent-sized instalments.

Surely if she made some regular payments the man would *have* to give her more time to pay the debt off? Ella's father should never have gone behind Jess's back in the first place, but that was typical of Peter Rosche.

And she could work from Dan's home. Of course she could.

'I'd like to help you.' Jess's fingers tightened around the handles of the stroller. 'I have some other children on Tuesdays and Saturdays, but I'd be willing to come to you the five other days, if you felt that could work for you. Ella would come with me, and I could give you a list of character referees.'

Not any family ones because Jess was alone in the world aside from Ella.

Her daughter started to fret in the stroller. 'Du, du, du-u-u!'

Jess leaned forward to unstrap her daughter and lift her out for a cuddle. 'Yes, sweetheart, we'll see the ducks now.'

Dan watched Jess cuddling Ella, and then he looked at his children and he lifted his youngest into his arms and started towards the duck pond. 'I could work around your Tuesdays and Saturdays.'

Dan told her how much he'd pay her per day. It was generous, even when he added, 'For that amount, I'd be asking you to remain there until I got home late some nights, but you and your daughter would have all your meals at my home.'

'It sounds very reasonable. I wouldn't mind doing that for you.' It sounded like a good way to save some money on her food bill, and Jess could drive the short distance back to her house at whatever time suited.

'Come and meet the children. That will be a good start, and . . . thank you. For approaching me and asking if I needed help.'

'You're welcome. It's nice to be able to help others.' Jess dropped a kiss onto Ella's head to hide the hope that wanted to force its way onto her face. Dan hadn't said he'd employ her yet.

But maybe he would. Maybe Jess would be able to help Dan while the money he paid her would help Jess.

Maybe Jess would be able to stop worrying, just a bit, and have enough money to stave off the wolves until she figured out something better for the longer term. Like tracking down Ella's father and making him take responsibility for setting her up for this fall?

Jess had tried to find Peter, just after Ella came along. He'd already disappeared by then.

Jess stuck her chin up. She could only try to sort things out, and she'd try with all her might. 'Righto, Dan. Take me to meet your children!'

CHAPTER TWO

'Kids, there's someone I'd like you all to meet.' Dan led Jess Baker to the duck pond where his children had been pretending not to watch him talking with Jess after Luke chipped them about their whispers.

The children were quite off the mark with their speculations. Jessica Baker was a great deal younger than him, not to mention those kinds of relationships should be kept out of the workplace.

Dan frowned. He simply wasn't interested in Jess. He might have noticed she was an attractive young woman, noticed her heart-shaped face, her slim straight nose, her honey-blond hair, those soft grey eyes, but he was not *attracted to her.*

And what mattered right now was that he needed to tell his brood that they'd be with a carer while he dealt with this business in Sydney. Deserting them when they'd only just arrived was the last thing Dan wanted to do, but he was going to have to do it.

Dan had a good business, but he was still a man with five children. He'd rented a house in Sydney and worked hard to save enough so they could buy their home out here, where things were cheaper and they could all enjoy a quieter lifestyle.

Jess Baker had told him her umbrella had bent bits, but something about the set of her chin suggested she might be a godsend, just the same.

'Luke, Rob, Daisy, Mary, this is Jess Baker.' Dan glanced at the child in the young woman's arms. He couldn't remember if Jess had said her daughter's name, yet he had no difficulty at all remembering the soft touch of Jess's fingers on his arm. He was . . . curious about her.

No. Dan wasn't curious. He was a father on his own with five children and eighteen years of memories of the one love of his life, and Jess was a very young woman and potential employee. Dan forced his gaze to Jess's daughter. 'And this is —'

'Ella.' Jess filled in the blank for him with a smile that transformed her face.

Rather than focus on that transformation, Dan gestured to the child in his arms. 'This is Annapolly. Her name's Pollyanna, but we started saying it the other way around and it stuck.'

Dan would simply push the confusing thoughts about Jess Baker away. And how could he think about reacting with awareness to this young woman anyway, when he hadn't done that about any woman at all for the last four years?

There'd been Rebecca for Dan since they were childhood sweethearts. They'd married, had the first four children. Partway through Rebecca's pregnancy with Annapolly, the doctors had discovered Rebecca had cancer. Rebecca had died a month after Annapolly's birth. Dan had just stopped with all that when he lost Rebecca.

'Hello.' Jess offered a uniform smile as her gaze shifted from one child to the next.

Rob responded with a curious, 'Hullo.'

'We saw you speaking with our father,' Daisy observed.

Mary asked hopefully, 'Are you gonna feed the ducks?'

'Yes.' Jess nodded. 'I am.'

Jess Baker was young, and she would come with her baby in tow, but Dan's instincts said Jess would be committed about the work. Those were the only instincts he needed to consider.

He pushed his thoughts into business mode. 'We'll have lunch at our new house.

It's a big farm-style home on a ten-acre allotment on the northern edge of town.' To his children he added, 'I'll explain what's happened with my work and how Jess has offered to help us on the way back to the house.'

Throw Jess into the middle. Let Dan see how she managed among the stacks of half-unpacked boxes and the children.

'Straight after the ducks,' Jess agreed, and handed out pieces of bread.

Dan's younger children gathered around. Luke and Rob didn't. They'd fallen into a whispered conversation. No doubt they had questions. Dan would answer them when he had everyone in the van, and hopefully there wouldn't be too much of an explosion when he told them they'd be in childcare for a fair chunk of their holidays.

Maybe they'd accept Jess's care easily. Maybe this would be all right. Maybe Dan's sea change for the children wasn't about to turn into a premature disaster before they even had a chance to give it a go.

Maybe?

And maybe Dan *would* be able to shove aside the way he'd reacted to Jess. He certainly wouldn't let it happen again. Dan failed to notice that, in thinking that, he had admitted to himself there *was* a reaction in the first place.

'Jess, I wonder if you'd mind sorting out lunch while I see to things with Roy, here?'

The Internet technician had arrived in his van as Jess Baker drove up in her small, older-model hatchback.

Dan spoke the words as he, the children, Jess, and the Internet technician trooped into the house. Dan had taken his moment to explain the childcare need to his children on the drive back here.

To allow them to moan and groan and then to make it clear there was no choice.

Now all Dan could do was see if Jess could manage. He'd made it clear he expected co-operation from the children with that.

'Of course, Dan. That's what I'm here for.' Jess's gaze darted this way and that. The kitchen was farther into the house, to the left through the open-plan living room. Jess spotted it and asked, 'Do any of the children have food allergies?'

'No.' Dan was lucky in that respect.

'Great.' The bow atop Jess's soft hair bobbed as she nodded her head.

Her clothes were bright and cheerful, and there were enough wooden bangles making their way up her arm that she could use them to start a small fire if she needed to.

Something about the combination of puckish face, bright clothing and the determined set of Jess's chin told Dan she might have lived more life than her youthful age suggested.

Right now she stood straight as an arrow with her baby perched on her hip while she looked around at the chaos inside the house. At least she didn't turn and walk right out again.

Dan didn't want her to go. He wanted a chance to get to know her.

What you want is a chance for her to look after the family while you're dealing with this work situation.

And if he tried to get to know her he might as well be getting to know an alien species. Jess Baker was a whole generation away.

'If you'll come this way with me.' Dan gestured the technician forward.

As they walked away Dan heard Jess say to his two eldest, 'How are your muscles? Do you think you could push those boxes into a line so they block that half of the kitchen? That way Ella will be safe while I make lunch.'

'Looks like you and the little lady have some chaos happening here.' The technician flipped the comment Dan's way as they

31

walked into the den.

'It's to be expected.' With another part of his mind Dan heard the first volley of questions from his curious younger offspring, and Jess's calm answers and the open and shut of cupboard doors as she looked inside. She wouldn't find much.

He had grossly overestimated how much unpacking one man and five excited children could get through in an evening and the following day. Dan had taken them into town to the park hoping to calm them down so he could come back and finish the work. Or at least get halfway there with it. 'Things are under control. Let's get this Internet connection sorted out.'

Roy set to work. A few minutes later he turned to Dan. 'There you go. The problem was this component.' Roy showed Dan the small box. 'I've replaced it. You won't be charged for this. I'll just send this one back.'

With that issue sorted, and Dan therefore connected once again to his working world via his computer, he thanked the man and let him out of the side door. Dan quickly jumped on to check his emails. There was just enough room to sit with the boxes shoved aside and stacked up.

'Lunch is ready, Dan. There's enough for an extra person —' Jess broke off as she glanced into the den.

She'd looked quite serious at first. Dan would even have said there were worried shadows in the backs of her eyes. Had those been there when they first met? Had he been too busy thinking about his own problems to notice? Were they related to caring for his brood?

Somehow he didn't think so, though that could prove to be challenge enough for her.

As Dan asked himself these questions those shadows were overshadowed by a teasing grin.

'Has the technician left,' she quipped, 'or did the boxes eat him?'

'I'm fairly sure he left. You managed something for lunch for everyone already?' Dan dragged his gaze from her smile. It was generous, open, and, yes, there *were* shadows in the backs of her eyes now that Dan took notice.

Dan cleared his throat. 'Was it really that long?'

'Ten minutes.' Jess shrugged her shoulders. 'The children pitched in.'

Utilise the troops. If Jess could settle them down a bit, even for a while, Dan would be grateful.

Since when do you need someone else to help? You spent the last two years turning your business into a work-from-home affair so you could do it all yourself. This shift is the final step, to give the kids the rural setting you talked about with Rebecca.

Dan had occasionally had to call on his sister Adele to help him out, but mostly he had his clients trained to understand that he worked from home and that was that. And his sister was travelling right now, taking time for *her* life.

Well, Dan wasn't going to regret this move. It was for the children, but it was for Dan, too. Lately the city made him feel as if he couldn't breathe. And his largest client undergoing an intensive pre-purchase examination wasn't something Dan could have anticipated. He hadn't even known they were thinking about a change of ownership!

He'd be fine, though. He shouldn't need to ask Jess Baker for help for more than a month or so.

'Thanks, Jess.' Dan drew a breath that didn't do a whole lot to ease the tight feeling that had formed in the centre of his chest as he started thinking ahead to leaving the children to get through most of their holidays without the fun and outings he'd planned for them. 'I'm guessing the kids are all hungry. I admit I am, too.'

Did Jess Baker eat more than enough to keep a sparrow going? She was small, slender. As she turned about the bright black-and-orange skirt swirled against legs that were tanned and sturdy.

Slender, but strong, then.

Dan lifted his gaze from her legs, and rapidly lifted it past other parts of her that seemed to catch his eye. 'I need to make those phone calls to your referees.'

More than that, he needed to stop noticing Jess in this way. He wanted Jess to work for him. And she was really young. And he . . . wasn't. And he didn't know a thing about her circumstances.

He had had his luck.

You haven't got over losing Rebecca.

He had, though. It happened four years ago. They'd all grieved and moved on. There'd been no choice. It was just that Dan knew he'd had more than his share. It would be impossible to love like that twice.

Meanwhile, there was Jess Baker, and . . . Dan stepped into the kitchen.

There was Jess's daughter playing with a set of plastic kitchen bowls in a makeshift playpen of packing boxes. There was Jess, handing out toasted cheese sandwiches and chocolate milkshakes.

Most of all there were five Frazier children

seated around the dining table, looking . . . at least relatively cooperative.

'I cut up the apple pieces.' Daisy gestured to a bowl in the middle of the table. 'Jess said if she watched me, it would be okay.'

Rob grinned with a chocolate milk moustache. 'I made the milkshakes.'

'And Annapolly and Mary worked together to put the plastic plates on the table.' Jess smiled and ruffled both little girls' hair before she passed Dan a plate of cheese sandwiches and sat with one of her own. 'We thought maybe after lunch we could try to get the kitchen and bathrooms sorted out.'

Right.

Dan drew a breath. 'I'm sorry, kids, that I've had to change our plans and that I'll be travelling to Sydney a bit for the next while and working long hours.'

'Yeah, well, some of us are way too old for a babysitter.' Luke muttered the words half beneath his breath.

But Dan still heard them and frowned, because they'd been over this in the car.

As Dan opened his mouth to chide his son, Jess spoke.

'You're quite right, Luke. I'm hoping I'll be able to rely on you and Rob to guide me with some of what's needed for the younger ones.'

Luke raised his gaze and for a moment seemed to fight himself before he unbent enough to allow: 'We can do that. There'll be heaps of stuff you don't know about them.'

Jess gave the boy a gentle smile. 'And maybe if we all work hard to get along and help your father be able to focus on his work, he'll manage a small outing with you all here and there?'

'Exactly what I'm hoping.' It was what Dan had been thinking.

There was a silence for a minute, and then Luke said, 'It's not your fault that you have to do this, Dad. You work hard to look after all of us. We'll just have to do things around here until you can do some stuff with us.'

Jess searched Luke's face for a moment before her gaze shifted to Dan. 'You must have been run off your feet since you got here, Dan. Probably everyone's feeling a bit out of sorts one way and another.'

Did she see the weariness that he'd been trying to hide from the kids for . . . Dan couldn't even remember how long?

'Yeah.' Dan cleared his throat. It had been hard to pack up their lives, to put the family photos away. He hadn't wanted to wrap up the pictures of Rebecca because he needed them in front of him and yet, since they arrived, that box had been the second last one Dan wanted to go anywhere near. The other held the urn of Rebecca's ashes.

Jess drew a deep breath and for a moment uncertainty flashed in the backs of her soft grey eyes. 'That is, if you're happy for me to continue, then I thought, as I said, we could do some unpacking after lunch.'

'I want to keep going.'

While the children finished their lunches, Jess showed Dan her written qualifications and gave him the phone numbers for her referees. 'Two are the mothers of the children I mind on Tuesdays and Saturdays.'

Today was Wednesday, so Jess had a couple of days before she would be with the other children again. 'The other referee is the woman who mentored me through training as a daycare mum.'

'Thanks, Jess.' Dan turned and headed for his den. 'I'll make sure I find time to make those calls this afternoon.'

The children pitched in to start sorting out rooms. Jess did her best to get everyone organised and help them all feel good about their achievements, and did well enough with the younger ones. Luke worked hard, but under his own steam and without a lot of communication. Jess would do what she could to draw the older boy out over time.

By mid-afternoon Jess's daughter had just woken up from her nap, Annapolly was parked in front of a children's programme on TV, and the rest of the children had gone outside with snacks to keep them going until dinner. Luke had placed himself in the role of supervisor out there.

'I hope you'll forgive me for disappearing and leaving you to it.' Dan had checked in with the family at intervals throughout the afternoon, but had taken the opportunity to work from his den as well. This financial examination was going to make its demands on his time.

He faced Jess across the kitchen table now and they both knew he had to give her his decision.

'I hope you were able to contact my referees.' Jess had tried to stay calm throughout the afternoon, but it hadn't been easy to beat back her worries about money.

'Your referees checked out fine.' Dan glanced about the now tidy kitchen. 'You've done wonders this afternoon.'

'Thank you. I welcome the chance to work hard.' Jess paused as her daughter crawled to her side. She picked her up and blew a raspberry kiss onto her neck.

Ella crowed and giggled.

Dan's gaze lingered on Jess's mouth before he quickly looked away, and Jess's heart skipped a beat. So much for controlling *that.* Apparently Dan could put paid to her efforts with a single glance.

Oh, why did she have to react to him like this? Be so conscious of him as a man when Jess had sworn off men and she'd meant it? Well, Dan didn't appear to want the attraction anyway so it would rapidly become moot, and that was *if* Dan kept Jess working for him.

'You're a natural mother, Jess. That much is very clear.' Dan hesitated, and then cleared his throat. 'Do you mind if I ask about other commitments? Will caring for my children interfere with other parts of your life?'

'There's just me and Ella, so there won't be interference from home with my work hours.' Jess drew a breath and slowly blew it out. Would he judge her for being a single mother?

'That's one less worry. I really need the help.' Dan straightened in his chair. 'Anything you can do towards housekeeping will also be appreciated.' He hesitated. 'I may be a little overprotective about checking in.'

Seeing that care in Dan touched a tender

place down inside Jess because Ella's father had proved so different.

'I'd want a contact number for you at all times, too.' She made sure her expression — a professional one — reassured Dan that all of his concerns were acknowledged. 'Also a complete list of medical conditions or special needs of the children. And I'd want to be paid weekly either by cash or bank cheque.'

If Dan assumed Jess would need to access her pay without a waiting period, he'd only be assuming the truth.

They sat there for a minute, sizing each other up. Jess looked over his ruffled dark hair and the hint of beard on his jaw, the shadows under his eyes that suggested he hadn't got a lot of sleep just lately.

And she said softly around her consciousness of him, 'I'd like to help you, Dan, if you feel I've passed the tests.'

'I don't mean to make it seem like that.'

Jess shook her head. 'If you hadn't grilled me, I'd have worried whether you were taking enough care of your children.'

'You're young.' The words were low.

'You don't look that old, yourself, you know.' He looked seasoned and appealing. Jess shook her head to try to drive the thoughts out.

41

Dan glanced from his daughter watching the TV, to the children outside, to Ella in Jess's lap, to Jess. 'Will you stick around for the rest of the day? And then I'll need you here first thing tomorrow morning so I can get on the road to Sydney.' He threw his shoulders back as though to say now the decision was made he'd stick by it and make it work.

Relief flowed through Jess. 'Thank you for giving me this opportunity.' She got to her feet and bent her head over Ella's so Dan wouldn't see the depth of that relief in her eyes. 'Just let me pop home and get Ella's playpen, monitor and walker and a few other things.'

They'd be fine working together. And this consciousness of him would be extremely transitory.

Of course it would!

CHAPTER THREE

'Why is it that parents make up stories about where babies come from?' The question was earnest, as were all of Daisy Frazier's questions. Daisy went on. 'And why would anyone believe those stories?'

It was early evening, the following day. Jess and the children were outside on the veranda that swept around three sides of the rambling home. Dan had unpacked like an automaton all yesterday afternoon and probably well into the night after Jess left that evening. Jess and the children had helped, too, of course.

The house was halfway habitable now, thanks to those efforts, but it was still nice to get outside. Jess had sliced up wedges of watermelon and brought everyone out here. The boys were having a seed-spitting contest.

Ella and Annapolly were playing with dolls. Mary, Dan's quiet six-year-old, was sitting on the edge of the veranda watching her brothers and swinging her legs.

That left Jess and ten-year-old Daisy, who was gifted with an inquisitive mind.

'Do you see Annapolly and Ella, Daisy?'

Annapolly was explaining to Ella in her childish way all about how the dolls were going on a road trip to get to a new house where they'd live happily ever after with a frog that laid golden eggs. Ella listened with awed attention, even though she didn't understand.

'Yes.' Daisy's brow wrinkled and she pushed her glasses up her freckled nose. She had dark hair like her father. They all did. Daisy had the same considering expression, too. 'What about them?'

'They're happy in their make-believe world. They can enjoy their imaginations and make up whatever stories they want.'

Daisy pondered for a second. 'If that's why kids want to believe that babies come from under a cabbage, or the stork drops them, I suppose it's okay.' She sniffed. 'But it would make more sense if they had a pelican drop them. Then they could tell themselves that the baby could be kept warm and safe in the pouch in the pelican's beak until it got dropped off.'

'They could.' Jess stifled a smile over

Daisy's pragmatic logic, and made a mental note to tell Dan this discussion with his daughter was coming, if it hadn't happened already.

Dan . . .

Despite his absence today, Jess had thought of him often. She'd asked herself how he was getting on in Sydney, had tried to remember whether he truly looked as handsome as she had thought on first meeting and again this morning when all of her awareness of him hadn't exactly been evaporated into oblivion.

Dan had phoned twice. Jess had assured him things were going well, and let whichever children had been hovering at the time have a quick chat to him. She'd at least attempted an attitude of professionalism on the surface.

After that second phone call Luke had tried to grill her almost aggressively about her personal life, why she was by herself and a few other questions that could have become a problem if Jess had let them. Instead, she'd stated only that being the mother of Ella was the greatest joy of her life and firmly turned the conversation elsewhere.

'Time to go in, I think.'

Ella was getting sleepy. Annapolly and

Mary were rubbing their eyes. Even the boys had lain back on the veranda floor after finishing their watermelon. And Jess had let her thoughts wander far enough. 'It's been a big day. Thanks for all trying hard today.'

There was the expected chorus from the younger ones of not wanting to go to bed but an hour later they were all in their rooms. It would be a while before some of them slept, Jess suspected, but she wouldn't be helping that if she hovered. She spent time doing chores and by then it was quite late and all the children were asleep. Well, she didn't know about Luke. His door was shut and she didn't feel she could intrude to check.

Jess curled up on the couch in the living room to rest until Dan got home.

She had five children and a baby to take care of tomorrow. The day after was Saturday and she had other children while their mothers worked at their Devonshire teas business.

Jess was an excellent daycare mum and trained to care for older children too. She would give that service to the very best of her ability; she would find her way forward with Dan Frazier's children. And when she got her first pay cheque she would go to the council and pay some money onto the overdue account there and talk to them about a more realistic payment plan. She didn't need to panic.

Things would be all right. And Dan would be back soon, and Jess *was* looking forward to seeing him. Just a little, and there was nothing wrong with that, provided she stuck to professional anticipation . . .

'Dan.' Jess spoke his name and sat up on the couch.

She'd been dozing when Dan unlocked the front door and stepped into the house.

'Hi. It's late. Sorry.' Dan's words were pitched low. He couldn't explain why they also emerged in a soft, deep tone. But coming home to find a woman sleeping, waiting for him, was something Dan hadn't done for years. Maybe the memory of that was what made him stop and take Jess in from the top of her head, with its messy cap of hair, to her bare feet with their high arches and purple painted toenails. It had to be memories, didn't it, even though Jess was nothing like Rebecca? He couldn't actually be truly attracted to Jess Baker.

'Was it very tiring, the trip into the city and the workload?' Jess's voice was soft and scratchy. Her cheeks had turned a gentle rose-pink as she met his gaze.

Because *she* was aware of *him?*

Rather arrogant to think such an appealing young woman would even notice you, Dan!

He took a step towards her. And then veered to the right to dump his briefcase on the couch because what would Dan do once he stood in front of Jess? Want to run his fingers through that fine, silky hair? Ask her to sit with him while he talked about his day? 'The financial examination process is very thorough. I won't mind not having to think about numbers until tomorrow.'

Dan needed to ask her about *her* work. How the children had fared today. He'd phoned in, but he wanted to hear more than those brief words. 'You'd ring me if there was a problem, not wait until I checked in?'

'Immediately.'

'I'll just look in on them. You don't mind? Then you can tell me how things went today overall. I don't want to hold you up from getting home.' He had to be businesslike about this.

'See them first, then I can give you a progress report.' Jess nodded. 'Ella's fast asleep in her travel cot. I can wait.'

Dan disappeared to the upper reaches of the house to check on his children.

In the living room, Jess watched his receding back until he disappeared from sight.

By the time Dan returned Jess had smoothed her hair. She didn't need to look like something that had been dragged backwards through a house, five children and a baby, she justified. She'd boiled the kettle and she tried to be very casual as she gestured, 'Would you like tea?'

That was suitably employee-like, wasn't it? And of course that was all Jess intended to be. Not that she'd been invited to be anything else. Not that she'd want to be invited.

Yes, you do.

No, you do not.

Dan smiled. 'At this point a good cup of tea would be worth crushing stones with my fingers for.'

Jess laughed, a low, startled sound that filled the kitchen and wiped Dan's face clean of the light-hearted expression that had accompanied his statement. In its place came the kind of tension that appeared in kitchens in the middle of the night when two people stood close together over a boiling kettle with nothing but silence around them. And a man's smile that had softened a girl's heart just a little more than she was ready for, so that she forgot to be careful and just enjoyed him for a moment.

Well, that kind of enjoying had to stop,

didn't it?

'I'll make the tea, then.' Jess swung about to get cups down from the cupboard.

'I'll get the milk from the fridge.' He gestured, as though maybe they'd both forgotten where the appliance stood in splendour in the corner of the room beside the dishwasher.

They put together their teas and carried them into the living room. Dan sat in a recliner.

Jess sat on the couch. She had a view of Dan in half profile. How could he look so gorgeous from every conceivable direction?

It must be the distinguishing effect of his age, Jess. You know — the age that means he's a whole generation older than you are and therefore completely unsuitable to be interested in. And that's not even mentioning the fact that you are working for him.

And then there was Luke's attitude. Jess could imagine how well something between his father and the new carer would go down with Dan's eldest son.

Maybe the boy still missed his mother and couldn't deal with the thought of Dan finding someone else.

Jess's heart softened at that, for how could she blame Luke for his grief?

'Mary's quiet. I'm working to draw her

out more. Rob likes to talk but I told him I have big ears, I can fit it all in.'

'You don't.' Dan uttered the words and dropped his gaze to his tea. 'Have big ears.'

'Well, no.' Jess cleared her throat as Dan lifted his cup to his mouth. She didn't bring up Luke. Jess would rather try to win the boy over, give it some time and see how things went. Instead, she broached the other potentially awkward topic. 'Daisy asked about how babies are made.'

Dan's cup shifted in a slight, involuntary movement before he carefully put it down. 'I see. Perhaps you'd better tell me.'

'Well, she's an inquisitive girl. It goes with her kind of intelligence, I think?' No need to blush over something that was as simple as pelicans versus storks. 'It's just, if you haven't already given her that talk, I think it might be a good idea if you did it quite soon. I know she's only ten, but schools are fairly forward about those issues these days, and Daisy's very curious. Today it was why other children believe in the stork and cab-bages. A week later it could be asking for an explanation about stem cell research or something equally tricky. I have a suspicion she might already know the, well, at least some of the mechanics about all that, so, you know —' Jess waved a hand '— maybe a father's perspective to help keep her comfortable as a child her age should be about the whole topic?'

Dan gave Jess one brief, trapped look. 'I can't ask you —'

To tell his daughter about it in a way that should come from a loving parent that Daisy trusted? Jess didn't want to even think about the topic while she was in the room with Dan and her heart was doing silly things in her chest.

But for Daisy . . .

'I could.' She bit her lip and rushed on. 'Talk to her, I mean.' The man was quivering in his boots at the thought of talking birds and bees with his daughter, not thinking about trying to investigate birds and bees with Jess.

Shut up, Jess. No, talk up. About Daisy. 'I could talk to her, but I really think this is something that needs to come from her dad.' She sought Dan's gaze and quickly looked away again. 'I think she might feel awkward talking with me about it.'

Jess drew a breath. 'Maybe once you've talked to her, you could get her a few books to read that explore related topics. Growing or waning numbers of children per family in various countries might be one area that could interest her. All sorts of things tie in with that. Politics, economics, religion.'

'Thanks.' Dan finally caught her gaze and held it. 'Aside from my daughter throwing you in the deep end, was everything else okay?'

'I think we all had a reasonable day, really.' Jess delved into another couple of issues with Dan, asked if he'd mind if she took them all into town tomorrow. It wasn't that far to walk and if they left early . . .

'That'd be fine provided you're comfortable the traffic won't be an issue if you're all on foot?'

He'd lived in a city.

Jess had, too, before she moved here. 'There's a pedestrian walk all the way from here into town. We'll stay on it, but traffic is always quite light anyway.'

He nodded. 'I'll be leaving for Sydney again early, but I'll have the weekend at home. Thank you, Jess, for taking this on to help me.'

Dan wasn't comfortable with needing her help, and his care for his children shone through in every word he spoke. Jess . . . well, she found that attractive about him. Probably not surprising when she'd been hurt by a man who had not only wanted nothing to do with recognising his baby, but had insisted on writing an agreement to silence Jess on the topic for ever.

She'd signed. By then she'd realised how little Peter Rosche had truly ever cared about her and that she couldn't expose Ella to how much her father didn't want her. Dan loving his children to pieces, yes, Jess did find that appealing, but she needed to admire it from afar, not want to acknowledge it on any kind of personal level.

'Do you know how to drive a van the size of mine, Jess? I'll fit the baby seat back into it tonight, for Ella. I still have ours from when Annapolly needed it.' Dan's gaze shifted over her, perhaps to assess whether he thought she could manage the larger vehicle.

Perhaps because, like Jess, he struggled not to notice her? To be aware?

In your dreams, Jessica Baker.

'I haven't driven a van like yours, but I've driven a four-wheel-drive.' Peter had owned one, and let Jess drive it now and then.

'I took the van today, but I've a second car in the shed here that I got shifted down with us.' Dan shook his head. 'I should have thought of that before I went to Sydney. You need the van here in case you have to drive anywhere with the children. You don't have to walk if you don't want to.'

'Thanks. That sounds sensible.' Jess got to

her feet. 'I'd better get Ella and head home.'

'Luke woke up when I checked on him. He said you let them have a watermelon-seed-spitting contest.'

Had the boy been accusatory about that? Jess paused a few steps away from the couch. 'Boys need to be a little bit gross, otherwise they don't know how to turn into men.'

Her eyes widened as she realised the way the words had come out. 'That is, I didn't mean it to sound as though men are gross. What I meant was —'

'Building strength by not having to act like girls all the time is important for the males of the race?' A smile twitched at the corners of his mouth.

This teasing style of grin was also a thing of beauty on Dan, Jess discovered, and she got caught in the headlights of it. Maybe that was because the smile reached all the way to the depths of his eyes even as it curved his lips in the most enticing way.

Home.

Now.

Before one more thought like that leaks from the one brain cell you have left, apparently, that's even trying to remain in control at the moment!

'I'll carry the baby for you.' Dan's smile

had faded, too.

Jess nodded and forced her feet to take her forward, into the room where Ella slept, bum in the air, in the travel cot. Jess scooped her daughter up and set her into Dan's arms in a smooth motion. Their hands barely touched and yet it was a touch that Jess had secretly craved.

Ella snuggled her sleepy head into Dan's neck and softness came over his face.

Jess swallowed hard. She walked ahead of Dan out to her car, opened it up and took over to settle Ella into her car restraint. 'Thanks for carrying her. I'll see you in the morning, bright and early.' *Sleep well, Dan.*

'Goodnight, Jess.' Dan rubbed his hand across his jaw as though uncertain what to do with it.

Reach for her?

In your dreams, Jess.

Jess started the car's engine and was grateful that it was a small, economic one that went a long way on its tank of petrol.

'You'll be all right going home at this hour?' Dan frowned. 'I want you to text me from your mobile phone when you get home. That way I can store the number to check on you the next time, and I'll know you got there okay.'

'Thanks.' It was the silliest thing, but Jess

had to turn her head away for a moment. She made a production of checking her blind spot and then she just rolled the car forward and drove away.

She had to do better at keeping her distance tomorrow, from Dan. Investing in his children was one thing. It was a part of the job, and that hadn't been completely easy so far. Luke had made sure of that.

Investing her feelings in Dan when he didn't want that and she couldn't afford to was a whole other matter.

'Not only can't afford it,' Jess muttered aloud as she turned the car into the cottage's driveway, 'I must not do such a thing. It's Jess and Ella and that's all. That's how it has to be.'

But Dan had been kind. Thoughtful. So much the opposite of the treatment Jess had received at the hands of Ella's father.

How was Jess supposed to deal with it?

By realising he'd been kind and thoughtful from an *employer's perspective.* That was how!

CHAPTER FOUR

'And my birthday's the eleventh of June.' Robert Frazier chattered beside Jess as she and all the children made their way back out of the council building in town the next morning.

They'd walked. It was a pleasant distance to the town centre from Dan's home; the morning was cool and fresh and the children had plenty of energy. Luke had wanted to stay home by himself but Jess had vetoed that.

At times Jess felt Luke was testing her. All she could do was try to be reasonable in return.

Jess had gained Luke's cooperation on this occasion and she had gone to the council to make her payment.

She just hadn't been able to get any better answers about the future of her home. She'd been given the runaround through three different people. She'd left Luke in charge while she did that, hoping the boy would soften if he realised she wasn't trying to treat him like a baby. Jess hadn't been able to tell whether her efforts with him had been successful or not.

Her efforts *hadn't* been particularly successful at the council. Well, she'd just have to go back when she only had Ella in tow and stick around until she got results. 'When we get home, Rob, we might make a chart of all the birthdays.'

Rob had already told Jess that Daisy's birthday was coming up. That was one to speak to Dan about when he got home later.

Jess shouldn't be viewing that discussion as the beginnings of a ritual, hoping for time with Dan regularly. 'Come on, kids. We'd better get back before the sun warms up too much and we don't feel like walking.'

After lunch Dan phoned and said he was coming home early and should see her mid-afternoon.

Jess got off the phone and found all the children in the living room.

'The laundry's all out on the line and I think I can get away with not doing too much else in the way of house cleaning for the day. Would anyone like to help make cookies?' Dan might like some home baking. Jess figured the kids wouldn't say no.

While Luke and Rob opted to ride their bikes outside, she got the others involved and set to work.

Soon there were cookies cooling on trays and Jess had handed some out to each of the children. The boys had come in for their share and life wasn't bad. Luke wasn't glaring right now. Jess had a job to do that she was enjoying. The children had cookies, and she wasn't totally out of money yet.

'Annapolly's taking a bit of time to use the loo.' Jess frowned. The little girl had gone to the bathroom just a few short minutes ago, but even so. 'Luke, would you take everyone out on the veranda to eat the cookies, please? I'll be there in a minute. I just want to check on your sister.'

Luke frowned, but wordlessly herded the others outside, and Jess turned her attention to seeking out Dan's youngest.

Independent loo visits for four-year-olds were important for feelings of pride and independence. Jess realised this and she didn't want to encroach on Annapolly's privacy. She didn't want to make unreasonable demands of Luke, either, and that was a whole other balancing act . . .

Jess strode towards the bathroom. Annapolly came out as Jess approached.

'There you are. I was wondering —' Jess

broke off.

The little girl's face was red and there were tears running down her cheeks.

'Oh, Annapolly, what's the matter?' Jess hurried forward.

It was then that she spotted the wadded bits of white in Annapolly's nose. Annapolly drew a breath through her mouth, a prelude to screaming, Jess suspected, and possibly to choking because her nose was blocked. 'Did you shove tissue paper in there?'

What if she inhaled it and choked herself? How far in had she pushed the paper?

Annapolly nodded miserably.

Jess had to fix this. Now. She took Annapolly gently by the shoulder, whipped a tissue out of her own pocket, held it out and said firmly, 'Blow that nose out, Annapolly. A good big blow until you've got nothing left.'

Annapolly blew. There were more tears, but there was also lots and lots of tissue paper. As Annapolly let out the first cry Jess scooped the little girl into her arms. Had it all come out? Had she damaged her nasal passages? Brought on the risk of infection, bleeding in there?

Jess hurried to the front door of the house. 'Everyone to the van, please. Luke, will you take Annapolly while I get Ella and her stroller? We're going to the hospital.'

'What did you let happen to her?' Luke asked the question fiercely.

'She filled her nose with tissue paper and may have harmed her sinuses.' Jess hurried away to get her daughter. The boy didn't need to accuse Jess of anything. Jess was already accusing herself.

The other children asked questions as Jess drove the van towards the hospital. Jess explained, and felt even guiltier as they all fell silent.

'I want to phone Dad.' Luke bit the words out. 'He has a right to know about this.'

'I was about to ask you if you'd do that. He phoned earlier and said he was on his way home. It would be good if he could meet us at the hospital.' Jess dug her mobile phone out of her pocket and passed it to the boy.

Luke tried but after a few minutes he'd had no luck.

'Will you text him, please, Luke, and ask him to come to the hospital? He might be in a low reception area but he should be close to home by now.' Jess didn't have time to wait for the luxury of Dan's opinion, or Luke's approval. She had to get Annapolly checked now. 'At least we're almost there.'

'She's all right, though.' Rob said it as

though he needed to believe it. 'We won't be leaving her there or anything.'

'No, we're not leaving her there.' Luke said this. 'She's coming home with us straight after, Rob. Don't be stupid.'

Jess might have chided the boy for the 'stupid' comment, but, if anything, Robert appeared reassured by his brother's harsh words, and Jess had enough to worry about right now so she left it alone.

The whole family fell silent as they stepped through the doors of the hospital's emergency entrance. Jess searched each face; saw their fear, Luke's fury and accusation. Behind his surly expression she saw Luke's fear, too.

Oh, Dan, what else have I added to your family's stress?

Why hadn't she just watched everyone more closely?

It was three minutes, Jessica, and you knew Annapolly had gone to use the loo. Filling her nose with tissue paper while she was there wasn't something you could have anticipated.

Maybe not, but it was Jess's job to anticipate, wasn't it?

Jess had Ella in the stroller. Luke had taken Annapolly into his arms. Jess eased the little girl from his hold and asked him to please watch his siblings while she spoke to the nurse. 'I may need to go into the examination room with her.'

'Dad had better get here soon.' With the brief words, Luke led the others to seats against the wall.

The lack of trust inherent in his statement didn't escape Jess.

'What have we here?' A friendly woman in her forties gestured Jess over.

Soon Annapolly was being examined. Her nose was declared to be sore, but the tissue paper was all out. No permanent harm had been done. The necessary germ-and-infection-repelling steps were taken. A few more tears were shed.

Jess could see the waiting room through the glass section of the doors and she saw when Dan arrived. There was a low-voiced conversation with Luke. The boy looked furious and was gesturing wildly. Dan also looked upset.

And the other children were all chattering at once.

They were probably telling Dan what a bad caregiver Jess had turned out to be, and they were right.

'You can go now, love.' The nurse looked at Annapolly. 'No more sticking things up your nose. Do you understand?'

'Yes.' Tears welled in Annapolly's eyes and

she held her arms out to Jess.

Jess cuddled the little girl and would rather have liked to join in with the weepies, at least for a moment.

Instead, Jess thanked the nurse and took Annapolly, and Ella in the stroller, out to the waiting room where Dan was in the process of trying to break away from his children, no doubt so he could come and find out about his daughter.

'Dan. I'm so sorry.' Jess handed Annapolly over. The little girl was already reaching for him. 'The nurse says there's no permanent damage. The others have probably told you what happened.' Jess explained what the nurse had done.

Annapolly *was* going to be fine, but right now her nose hurt and that was Jess's fault. Dan would sack her for this, and Jess would deserve it because she'd let Annapolly get out of her sight and hurt herself.

'Let's all go home.' Dan's gaze went from the daughter in his arms to the other children. 'Hospitals —' He didn't say more, just hustled everyone outside.

Jess drove the van back home while Dan drove in his other car, Annapolly, Luke and Rob with him.

Jess *never* lost track of a child when she looked after them at the cottage. She supervised *everything.* Well, she'd failed to do that at Dan's house, hadn't she?

When both vehicles stopped outside the house a few minutes later Daisy took Annapolly by the hand and said the little girl could come and lie on her bed with her and she'd read to her. Mary went with them.

Luke and Rob had still been talking to their father when the car pulled up. Rob disappeared outside to ride his pushbike and Luke cast a furious glance in Jess's direction before he turned back to his father. 'I don't like her. I don't want her here. She can't even take care of everybody and you seem to think the sun shines out of her, Dad. You don't even know her.'

He got on his bike and rode off to the far reaches of the property before Dan could do more than start to rebuke him.

That left Jess, Dan and Ella, who'd fallen asleep on the way back. Jess changed her and put her down to nap in the travel cot and went back to face Dan. There was nothing else for this but to take full responsibility and hope Dan could get over her negligence enough to trust another person with his children. She didn't know what to do about Luke. He would end this short association disliking Jess.

Well, Jess would just have to accept that,

she supposed.

Dan was in the kitchen.

'You're eating cookies.' Jess blurted the words with a complete lack of comprehension.

'They're very good cookies. I don't get home baking like this very often and since my eldest just did his best to make sure I have a three-day heartburn, anyway, I think I deserve them.' Dan took another cookie and, with his other hand, poured two cups of tea. His mouth was still tight. 'Potato crisps are my usual addiction. I can go through packets of those in a day. I'm surprised the children left any cookies for me.'

'We'd only just got them all out of the oven when we had to leave for the hospital.' Jess glanced around her. She'd spotted empty crisp packets in Dan's den and thought it was the children. 'I didn't tidy up, just rushed out.'

'No, there tends to be a sense of panic.' He said it as though he knew. Dan handed her one of the cups of tea. 'Sit down, Jessica.'

Jess sat. She didn't think she could drink the tea, yet she found herself sipping the sweet brew and taking comfort from its warmth. But Dan. Why wasn't Dan yelling?

Or very cold towards her? Something?

'You're going to sack me kindly but there's no way anyone is to blame but me.' That knowledge stabbed right through Jess's heart. 'I let Annapolly go to the bathroom and left it several minutes before I thought about the fact that she hadn't come back. You must have been worried when you got Luke's text message.'

'I don't know what's got into that boy —' Dan broke off, drew a tight breath and started over. 'I was worried.' His jaw tightened. 'And I admit, I did feel angry for a minute when I realised you were all at the hospital. I wanted to blame you for not watching them properly, for potentially risking harm to one of them.'

As Luke had blamed her. Well, in this case Luke had the right of it. Jess forced herself to sit straight and not lower her gaze. She deserved this. Every bit of chewing over that Dan needed to hand out. 'You have every right to be angry.'

'What I am is human, Jess.' Dan rubbed his hand over the back of his neck. 'I pushed my worry out into irrelevant anger for a brief moment. But the fact that Annapolly stuffed her nose with paper doesn't make you a negligent caregiver, no matter what my overactive mind might have tried to tell me to the contrary.'

Jess barely took in his words. 'I'm the one —'

'Who had to deal with the drama this time.' Dan shook his head. 'There's five of them, Jess. They range in age from four up to fifteen. It's a big house. No matter how good you are at your job there'll be times when more than one of them is where you can't see them. I do understand that. As their father, I *live that* on a daily basis. You can't tie them all to chairs in the kitchen all day. And I asked you to help out with housekeeping and other duties as well.'

'I guess so.' Jess frowned. 'Luke wanted to be left here by himself this morning and I wouldn't agree. I didn't think you'd want that.'

'No.' Dan put his tea down and leaned forward to face her across the kitchen table. His hazel eyes searched her grey ones. 'Annapolly is more than capable of using the bathroom on her own. You let her do that. She pushed tissue paper into her nostrils while she was in there. She came out in distress, you got her to blow it out and took her to the hospital to make sure there was nothing still lodged up there and to find out whether any serious damage had been done.'

He reached briefly to touch Jess's hand. 'I'm not sacking you, Jess. It was an accident, and Annapolly is okay. In the end that's what counts.'

He wasn't going to sack her. Dan wasn't furious. He'd had his bout of anger and that had been because of fear.

'Thank you.' Jess's words were husky with relief, and with consciousness of Dan's determination to be fair.

And of Dan himself . . .

And because that was so very unwise, she got to her feet.

Dan stood at the same time and Jess looked at him, overwhelmed for a moment. 'I'll work harder to keep a better watch on things in the future.'

Dan searched her face. 'You're all right about it now?'

No, she wasn't, but Jess *would* be all right. She would make that be so, somehow.

Maybe Dan read her confusion and uncertainty. Maybe he forgot for a moment that she wasn't one of his children in need of a comforting hug, because somehow his arms had opened and Jess was inside them with her nose pressed to his chest.

Jess was enveloped by the solid feel of him, of his broad shoulders making a protective curve while he drew her close to his body. There was tension in Dan's body. More when Jess wrapped her arms around him and hugged him back.

Maybe she shouldn't have done that, but she did, and their hug changed right at the end to something that wasn't entirely about comfort.

'I'll pack the rest of the cookies away into a tin.' Jess spoke the words with the length of the kitchen between them. She'd got herself out of Dan's arms and a distance away very quickly. She shouldn't have hugged him in the first place.

'Just as soon as I've checked on everyone.' She cleared her throat. 'Thanks, Dan, for your kindness and understanding. There won't be a repeat where you have to come to the hospital, because of something like this.'

Jess would make sure of it. He didn't need that. Jess wasn't so foolish that she couldn't imagine that Dan would have had to go to a hospital or more than one, when his wife died.

Jess didn't know what had been wrong with his wife or how she had died, but she'd seen how the children retreated into worried silence in Randurra's emergency department this afternoon. Some of Luke's anger had been about that, too, Jess suspected.

And she couldn't have stayed within that embrace. Not without risking Dan realising how it was impacting on her. They had a working relationship and needed to stick to it, for so many reasons! 'And I'd like to take the children back to the hospital very soon for a visit. We can take a gift to donate to the children's ward. It'll be a chance for the kids to see a brighter side of the hospital.'

Dan murmured an agreement. Jess hoped she could convince Luke to agree to this. She went to check on the girls, and then Dan's sons. Rob was fine. Luke was playing a computer game in his room, screeching a racing car around corners on the screen. Would that help him get out his aggression? Should Jess try to speak to him?

She knocked on his door and waited for his head to turn. 'Luke —'

'Dad told me you're staying.' He'd paused the game for the moment it took him to speak the words. 'Doesn't mean I have to like it.'

'No. It doesn't mean that.' Jess pushed back a sigh and left him to it.

When she came back, Ella was stirring in the travel cot and Jess got her up and took care of her needs and set about watching over everyone while she organised a meal. Everyone except Luke, who was still in his room.

Annapolly was okay. And Jess still had a job. She was more than grateful about that. Dealing with Dan's eldest was no doubt going to be even more difficult now, but Jess wasn't about to give up. She could see a good boy in there beneath Luke's aggression.

And the reason for his aggression, Jess? The fact that he didn't like the vibe he noticed between you and his father? What about the fact that vibe hasn't gone away?

In the end, it would be irrelevant and Jess had to hope that Luke would see that eventually. Whether Jess was aware of Dan as a man or not and even if Dan was aware of her as a woman, it wasn't something that could or should be pursued between them.

If Jess thought that Luke should allow his father to do whatever he wanted when it came to women, she was smart enough to know that she should not interfere.

Dan watched Jess settle his family in for the evening. She'd whipped up a meal for everyone while she kept a close eye on what all the children were doing, and kept her baby daughter happy, but he could see the tension was still within her.

Rebecca had looked just as devastated after the first trip to the hospital over a hurt child.

But Jess wasn't Rebecca, wasn't anything like Dan's late wife. Dan had hugged Jess because she'd looked as if she needed it, and he had rapidly realised the hug could easily have become more for him. He'd wanted so much to kiss her.

While Jess had broken out of his arms and distanced herself physically, Dan had worked to distance himself mentally. He wasn't happy to be attracted to Jess. Now wasn't the time for his libido to wake from hibernation and start giving him trouble. But it must only be physical awareness because his emotions were still with Rebecca. Well, no, of course they weren't, not in that way because Rebecca was gone and he'd grieved, but . . .

After the numbness and slogging through the days until the kids had got on their feet again, Dan now only wanted to focus on the children and his work. He *needed* to do that. He had nothing for anything else.

And Luke was being a complete pain about the whole topic, and that made Dan really uncomfortable. He hadn't thought about how his children might react if he wanted to start seeing a woman; it hadn't been something he'd expected to happen. It still grated to have Luke behaving so aggressively and taking a dislike to Jess when in Dan's opinion she didn't deserve it.

Yes, there'd been Annapolly's mishap, but Luke knew as well as anyone that accidents happened, and he'd started to be difficult before today's incident.

Well, Dan had told his son to pay Jess appropriate respect, and when the dust of today's issues had settled a bit he would check to see if that was happening. There was no point taking it further, because Dan *wasn't* seeking anything but a working relationship with Jess.

As she got the children sorted out after dinner and ready for bed Dan turned his attention to work. Right at the moment he didn't have a whole lot of choice about that either!

'I'm leaving now, Dan.' Jess made the announcement from the doorway of his den. She looked ruffled and still uncertain of herself. She had Ella fast asleep in her arms. 'Thanks for fitting that baby restraint to the van before you left this morning. Oh, and I did want to bring up Daisy's birthday.'

'You're welcome.' He drew a breath. 'Daisy's birthday is next week.'

'Yes. I can make a cake, if you like.'

'That would be nice.' He cleared his throat. 'Her gifts are purchased, as are most of the birthday party supplies. What I can't provide is any extra children for the party. There hasn't been time yet or the opportunity to find any new friends for them here.'

Dan hesitated and then shook his head. 'That's not something I can do in the next few days, but a family party will still be fun for Daisy. I'll see you Sunday, then.' If he walked her to her car he'd do something irrational. Such as try to talk about things that were only going to make both of them feel awkward.

'I'll send a text to your mobile when I get home.'

'Goodnight, Jess.'

'Goodnight, Dan.' She walked away with Ella clasped in her arms. A slip of a girl who was the mother of a baby, but she was not the mother of any of Dan's babies.

So he would get some sleep and Jess would go home and get some sleep and look after her other children tomorrow. When she came back to Dan on Sunday she would have recovered from knowing that Annapolly hurt herself while under her care. Hopefully by then Luke would have a better attitude to life as well.

Dan went back to his workload at the computer and made sure his mobile phone was nearby so he would hear it when she sent her text message through to say she had arrived home safely.

He drew a packet of potato crisps from the stash in his drawer. He would make a list of what needed to be done for Daisy's birthday party, and when Jess came back on Sunday they would go through it and work it all out.

Dan and Jess, because that was what he was paying her to do.

And only that. Dan ate a few more crisps and wished he didn't feel so run-down as he tried to think about it all.

CHAPTER FIVE

Days passed. The trips to and from Sydney were tough. Long hours on the road, longer hours of hard work for his client company. Days at home without Jess's help meant working into the night to catch up time lost during the day. Dan pushed on. He didn't have a whole lot of other choice but he'd bought himself time for today.

His most academic child was eleven years old and Jess had worked miracles for the party. Dan glanced about the backyard. It wasn't an enormous crowd but it was one that was bringing Daisy happiness.

'Oh, Daisy, that's a really cool birthday present. I don't think I'd be allowed to have that for my birthday.' The comment came from a girl Daisy's age as his daughter unwrapped the birthday present Dan had bought for her.

The birthday group consisted of Daisy's brothers and sisters, Dan, Jess, Ella and three local girls who would be in the same school year as Daisy when she started at the public school a month from now.

Jess had found some potential playmates for Daisy.

'Dad lets me have things because he knows I'll be responsible with them.' Daisy spoke the words with a smile.

Dan returned that smile. 'Chemistry sets need to be used under careful supervision, but I think you'll enjoy it, Daisy.'

'You do well with her, Dan.' Jess made the comment from Dan's side. 'A chemistry set was a great idea for her.'

'Thanks.' Dan turned to look at Jess, and for once really *allowed* himself to look. Today she wore a floral print skirt teamed with a black sleeveless top, big wooden hoop earrings and a chunky wooden necklace. She looked young and vibrant and beautiful.

And Dan was pushing forty, a father of five growing children. What on earth did he imagine Jess might see in him when she could have any man of any age? She would probably only *want* a man much closer to her own age. Why even ask the question anyway?

Because you know you are attracted to her.

Well, he could just become unattracted.

And right now Jess not only looked gorgeous, she also, behind her cheerfulness, seemed a little worried or . . . scared?

If that had anything to do with her work for him, Dan needed to know. Was Luke making things difficult for Jess still?

Jess lit the candles on the cake.

'You have to make a birthday wish before you blow out the candles, Daisy.' Another of the little girls made this suggestion as they all crowded closer. 'You can come to my house for my birthday, too. It's in March.'

'Thanks.' Excitement dawned in Daisy's eyes. 'I'd love to do that.'

Daisy blew out her candles. She even closed her eyes first.

The wheel of a baby walker butted against Dan's foot. He glanced down and straight into a pair of soft grey eyes so like Jess's. Ella smiled up at him.

'Well done, Daisy,' Jess said.

Was Jess working very hard not to be aware of Dan, or was he imagining it? Dan needed to stop such thoughts whether they were right or not.

Jess went on. 'Time to dish up this cake and see if it turned out as well as I hoped.'

Jess had baked and decorated the cake last night. She was dedicated to her job. She handled the basics of the housekeeping with apparent ease, too, and that had taken a load off for Dan.

It had made him wonder if he could have a housekeeper on a permanent basis. He'd been busy saving to move the family, and he probably hadn't really wanted the interference anyway but with Jess . . .

Dan had enjoyed having her in the house. Especially on the days he'd worked from home.

Not good thoughts to have, Dan Frazier. She's the daycare mum who has also generously helped out with housekeeping and cooking, and that's all she should be to you.

'Would you like the treasure hunt now, Daisy? Excuse me.' Jess slipped past Dan to start supervising the activity. The hem of her skirt brushed against Dan's leg. Dan looked at a piece of bright fabric against his denim cut-offs and he breathed in and caught the scent of her perfume warmed against her skin and wanted . . .

'Ah, let me just give you some room.' Dan shifted back, and Jess's head dipped until all he could see was the fan of her lashes against her skin, and he knew Jess was just as aware of him as he was of her. If he kissed her, maybe he would be able to figure out why —

Dan's mind froze as the thought registered.

Jess moved away and the party went on around them, but from that point on Dan couldn't go anywhere near her without being conscious of her.

And from the way she kept avoiding his gaze, she was equally conscious of him.

Two hours later parents started arriving to collect their children, and soon after it was just Fraziers and Jess and Ella.

Dan turned to Daisy. 'Now that the party's over would you like to rest for a bit, or are you busting to get into your chemistry set?'

Daisy gave him a considering look. 'I'd like to read the books that came with it, first. And we don't want to start anything with that set while Mary and Annapolly are around. I think we'll need to use it after they've gone to bed at night, Dad.'

'Oh, clever work, Daisy.' Jess, who'd been tidying paper plates and plastic cups off the long trestle table, spoke softly beneath her breath so only Dan heard. 'Care for your sisters *and* negotiation for a later bedtime, all rolled into one.'

She turned quickly aside, but not before Dan saw the smile that crept to her face.

Dan cleared his throat. 'We'll discuss that later, Daisy.'

Daisy went off to read, and Mary and An-napolly played with leftover wrapping paper and pieces of ribbon. Jess warned them not to stick anything into their noses but An-napolly had learned that lesson.

Ella was still in her walker and Jess and Dan started in again on the mess.

Dan said abruptly, 'Daisy's eleven now, and I let Rob have an extra hour at that age.'

'Yes, of course. You know what you're do-ing, Dan.'

Jess pursed her lips and nodded soberly, while her eyes danced and the big wooden hoop earrings danced and that damned necklace sat between her breasts and kept drawing Dan's gaze.

'Thanks for finding some girls her own age to come to her party.' Dan all but growled the words, but he meant them, just the same.

'I knew one of them already and she was more than happy to bring two of her friends.' Jess's face softened. 'I'm glad they seemed to get along with Daisy.'

Dan shoved his hands in his pockets and glanced about the big yard at the party remnants. Even the tree cubby house was decorated in streamers. Jess had asked him to purchase them and then let the kids loose to make things festive.

'If you need to work, Dan, I can keep going here.' Jess glanced at the three little girls as she spoke. 'They're all content for the moment.'

She followed Dan's gaze to the tree house. 'This sure is a great home for children. I'd like to explore the rest of the property one day, though I guess they'd all need to be in the right mood.'

Dan could be in the right mood. In fact, Dan was in *too much* of a right mood at the moment. 'I'll help you clean up.' He couldn't just leave her with all of it, Dan justified.

They worked together to clear away the aftermath of the birthday party. Jess disappeared periodically to check on one or other of the children. She was being very vigilant in that respect and Dan suspected she still felt guilty over Annapolly's episode with the tissue paper.

Dan took out the trash and glanced up from the task and there was Jess on the veranda, lifting her daughter into her arms while she said something to Luke who'd been about to ride past her on his bicycle.

Dan's eldest gave Jess a sullen look and then cast one in his father's direction as well, and rode away. Luke needed to mend that attitude because Dan didn't want Jess leaving thanks to the boy being unreason-able.

I want to keep her working here so she's always around.

The thought pushed into Dan's mind, pushed past four years of defences and a lot of buried grief and just lobbed into his brain. Not his heart, though. This tightness that he had so often in his chest, that wasn't about Jess. That had started long before Dan met her. If there were other responses inside his chest right now that did relate to Jess, well, they were because she was work-ing out so well for the kids.

'I just put Ella down for a nap. I think all the excitement today wore her out.'

Jess had joined him in the kitchen. He hadn't even realised he'd gone inside and had been standing there, staring into space. Thinking about the past and thinking about Jess.

'I don't know about your life. Except that you're raising your baby on your own, and you're proving to be good for my children.'

'I'm enjoying caring for them.' Jess bit her lip. 'Trying not to crowd them, but to keep a close enough eye on all of them at the same time. Trying to win Luke's trust. He's still angry over what happened to An-napolly, and . . . well, I'm not sure what

85

else is bothering him. I think the birthday party came off well, anyway.'

'It did, and Luke is just going to have to settle down.' Dan didn't want to think about the reasons for Luke's attitude. If Luke thought he had the right to decide Dan couldn't have a social life, he was wrong about that.

It wasn't the issue, here, but . . .

Dan pushed the thoughts away. 'Jess, will you tell me about your family? Where you grew up and what brought you here to Randurra?' Maybe if he understood Jess better, that would help him to guide Luke as well.

Or simply make it more difficult for you to keep your interest in her on a professional footing.

For a moment she was silent and then she drew a big breath and turned to search his eyes. 'I grew up in Wollongong, so not too far from Sydney, really. My parents died when I was small. I don't remember them. An older aunt raised me and she passed away during my last year of high school. I worked in a few casual jobs after high school until I decided to become a certified day-care mum.'

She hesitated before she went on. 'While I was expecting Ella, I came here to

Randurra.'

A fierce expression came over her face. 'I'm going to make sure my daughter has security and love for as long as she needs it in life. That she's always got me and doesn't feel abandoned.'

As Jess had felt alone because of her loss of family?

Dan had been telling himself they had nothing in common but there was this . . .

Had she chosen to be a daycare mum as a means of trying to fill that lack of family in her life? 'Your vocation —'

'Is something that I truly enjoy. I adore children, and I know there are plenty of parents who want to work while their children are small, or need to. That's a personal choice. It's just, for myself, I'd prefer to keep Ella close by.'

Jess turned the conversation to Dan. 'What about you? You came here from Sydney, but what about your life before that? Do you have other family?'

'There's my sister and brother-in-law. Dad passed away ten years ago and Mum retired to Queensland. I see her about once a year.'

Jess nodded. 'And the children's mother . . .'

'Her name was Rebecca.' Dan drew a breath. It wasn't as though it was difficult

87

to talk about her. He'd done so with the kids so many times.

Yet his chest still hurt, unexpectedly so when he looked into Jess's soft, understanding eyes. 'I loved her from when we were teenagers. We were together for eighteen years. She . . . got cancer while she was pregnant with Annapolly and the specialist team believed there'd be time to treat it but I lost her a month after the birth. That was four years ago.'

The moment Dan said it, he wondered if he should regret it. He didn't bare his soul to others, and the loss of Rebecca was something that was in his past now. He'd grieved and got on with his life, so why did it hurt so much to admit what Dan had known from the start? That Rebecca *had been* his chance at love and he . . . hadn't had enough time with her?

Jess didn't recoil. Instead, understanding and something that wasn't envy but perhaps longing flashed across her face before she quickly dropped her gaze. When she looked up again, her expression was guarded. 'I'm sorry for your loss, Dan. Thank you for telling me how she died. I don't think I mentioned that I took the children back to the hospital. We just dropped off a small gift to the children's ward. I think that was a good balancing experience for all of them.'

'Daisy told me about it.' Dan acknowledged her words with a dip of his chin, and
wondered how his exploration into understanding Jess Baker had turned into an ex-
posé of his own thoughts. 'What I really
want to know is if you're okay, Jess? Sometimes I see worry in your eyes.'

She blinked, and blinked again and something in her face seemed to tighten before
she threw back her shoulders and stuck out
her chin. 'I'm okay, Dan. Of course I am.'

But Jess wasn't, not entirely. So what
wasn't she telling him?

Dan pondered that question again the
next day as he dug out the box of family
photos and started to put some on the walls.
The urn with Rebecca's ashes was still in its
box.

The pictures felt somehow different. It
must be the new house. And if Jess said she
was fine, then he had to believe her. Didn't
he?

Dan buried himself in his work. Over the
following days he was able to scale down
the amount of time he was spending in Sydney, but the hours were still long. When he
felt tired he ate packets of crisps. He barely
even thought about Jess being around all
the time, or listened for her voice while he

was working, or enjoyed checking in with her when he stepped out of his den to see how the children were getting along.

Right, Dan. That's exactly how it is.

Well, at least he seemed to have convinced Luke that he was only interested in how Jess cared for his family, and Jess seemed to be making progress whittling down the boy's defences.

Days went past with Jess feeling way too conscious of Dan. Why did it have to be like this when he had told her how much he'd loved his wife? Surely she had nothing left inside her when it came to trusting a man, and it was clear she could never compete with Dan's Rebecca, even if she wanted to.

'I think I'm confused.' Jess muttered the words at a pile of clothing as she shoved it into the machine in the laundry room.

Maybe she needed to believe that not every man was selfish and uncaring like Peter, Ella's father. Maybe that was all.

Oh, yes? And that fact alone made her pulse race every time she thought of Dan, or looked at him?

'Jess, I wanted to ask if you'd like —'

'Oh. Dan. I didn't realise you were there.'

He had his glasses on his nose, so he must have been working on the computer in his den. And he was so close. Jess could reach out and trace the grooves beside his mouth with her fingertips, or caress his ruffled dark hair.

And Dan could be totally resistant to all of the above, because she was his employee and not in his age bracket and he *had been* resistant to being aware of her, right from the start.

'Oh. Um . . .' *Think, Jessica. About something* other than *how delectable he looks.* 'What — what did you want to ask me, Dan?' Even saying his name sent a thrill through her.

They were in a house full of children. Anything else aside, no thrills were allowed!

Dan's gaze shifted over her face, the bright pink bandanna tied through her hair, down over the loose cream cheesecloth blouse and darker pink skirt and back up to linger on her lips before it finally came back to meet her eyes.

'We, ah, I've got a two-day gap where there won't be much happening with the situation in Sydney. I want to take the family to the beach.'

Right. Dan wanted to go away to the beach with the children. Jess would lose two days of being around him.

You'll lose two days' work. Remember you

91

still haven't managed to get Lang Fielder to agree in writing to any extra time to make the repayments.

Jess had managed to see the man. He'd said she should go on making what payments she could out of her wages with that negotiation in mind. It wasn't enough of a reassurance.

Well, Jess didn't want Dan to see her fear. She had learned from being scammed and written out of his life by Peter Rosche that she had to stand by herself. For her sake and for Ella's sake, too. Jess *needed* to remember that. 'That sounds like a lot of fun. I'm sure they'll all enjoy it. When were you planning to go?'

'Tomorrow.' Dan said the word in a low, deep tone.

'Tomorrow.' Jess repeated the word on a breath before she remembered she needed to comprehend it, not merely say it. 'Right, well —'

'Would you be available to come with us? You and Ella? I've picked days when you don't have to mind other children.' Dan backed out of the room as though he'd belatedly realised they were hovering in there, close, quiet, *together*.

Just as Jess had realised it.

He went on. 'You don't have to, but it'd

make it easier for me. Two sets of adult eyes to watch them around the water.'

'For the children's sakes.' That was easy. *And* Jess could let herself be relieved about the pay as well. 'It's always better to have two adults with that many children and water involved.'

Jess had never taken Ella to the beach. But with Dan, she could go.

And spend two days of sun, surf and sand with a gorgeous man.

Oh, for heaven's sake. She'd just gone over this and they would be surrounded by children. There would be sand in shoes and hair and clothing, but there would certainly *not* be romance in the air.

'I'll be happy to make the trip with you, Dan.' Jess stuck her chin out. Way out. So far out that even she couldn't miss the fact that this was a statement about her work for Dan, not about wanting to laze on a beach with him.

Dan pushed his glasses up his nose, seemed to realise they were there, and whipped them off. 'I'm glad. I'll feel better about it.'

'I will too, Dan.' Maybe the couple of days away would help Jess think her way forward with the situation regarding her home.

If not, then she needed to start knocking

on the other half of Randurra's doors, and hope that a great deal of lucrative work came to light as a result. Work she could do around her current two jobs.

And really, who needed sleep or rest, anyway, provided she could make sure Ella was happy, and keep getting more money to pay off the debt? As Dan preceded her, Jess made her way out of the laundry room. 'I'd better speak to everyone about packing for the trip.'

CHAPTER SIX

'Everyone ready for this trip to the beach?' Jess had supervised visits to the bathroom for the younger ones, and waited while various Fraziers ran around needing this item and that item that they simply couldn't leave behind for their trip.

She'd packed for herself and packed for Ella and checked what had been packed for the children.

Rob had wanted to bring half the house for playing with on the beach. He'd settled on two soccer balls, and a whole tube of tennis balls.

The girls wanted to collect seashells, so buckets for them.

And Jess had packed the spades because once they got there she assumed at least one of them would want to make a sandcastle.

Just as well it was a big van. Jess strapped Ella into her travel seat and waited while

Fraziers piled in all around her daughter. Watched bouncy bodies and an abundance of energy until she saw for herself that everyone had seat belts fastened. Luke was the only sober one, and that didn't surprise Jess. She was doing what she could to befriend the boy, but he still treated her with suspicion and distrust half the time.

Then Luke dug Rob in the ribs with his elbow and challenged him to a race along the beach once they got there, Rob laughed and agreed and both boys smiled, and Jess really relaxed for the first time in ages.

Ella was kicking her legs and wiggling. Jess climbed in the front beside Dan, glanced at him and a big, silly grin spread across her face. She pushed her floppy hat off her head and let it dangle by its strings down her back. 'We're going to the beach.'

'Right after we stop in town for the things I know they'll all start asking for ten minutes up the road.' Dan's gaze took in the floppy hat, her face. He watched her strap herself in and his eyes came back up to briefly catch hers again.

How did he do that? Simply look at her and make her world shift? He probably meant absolutely nothing by it.

Jess took the hat completely off. 'Stopping is good. For what the children might want.'

Jess needed to stop fixating over Dan, and how good he looked in a navy polo shirt that set off the tan of his arms and khaki knee-length cut-offs that accentuated his thigh muscles.

'We'll have to be careful with sun block and staying off the beach during the worst hours of the day.' The words were primmer even than Mary Poppins could have been.

Jess didn't have a beach umbrella, but Dan had three tossed into the back of the van.

The younger children started chattering, asking their father questions and firing a few at Jess as well. Jess answered, and she drew a deep breath, which didn't help because Dan was wearing a really nice aftershave lotion.

'Jess?'

From the tone of Dan's voice, Jess suspected he might have asked her something already — and she'd been too busy daydreaming about sniffing his neck to hear it.

'I'm sorry, Dan. What did you say?' Jess glanced through the windshield and realised they'd come to a stop outside the town's supermarket. 'Oh. Shall I go in for the things? Do you have a list? Or did you want me to mind the children, or is everyone going?'

'We're all going,' Rob chimed in and then there were Frazier children bailing out of the van at the speed of light. 'We do this every trip. It's fun.'

Dan got Ella out of her seat and held her and they all trooped into the supermarket. The children proceeded to select one family-sized bag of crisps or sweets each, but first fell into discussion over what things they weren't having because didn't Mary remember getting sick eating those last year? And it wasn't a good idea for Rob to eat ones with yellow food dye because he got even more hyper than usual.

And then Luke seemed to realise that he was acting like a child, and took his bag of crisps, went to the checkout by himself, bought them and left the store.

Jess chewed her lip. 'Should I go after him, Dan?'

'Let him go.' Dan watched his son leave the store. 'He needs his space sometimes.'

Jess realised she had grown accustomed in this short time to the sense of family she received while caring for Dan's children. She didn't know how she'd been given the gift of becoming part of this, even if it was only for a few weeks or so.

She didn't want to lose her cottage and maybe have to leave Randurra to find different work, and not see Dan or his family again. There. She'd admitted both fears and what good had it done her? Jess was doing what she could about the cottage. And she didn't want these confused reactions and thoughts about Dan and her sense of family. Jess didn't *have* a sense of family except Ella, and that was everything to her.

'What would you like, Jess?' Dan gestured to the shelves. 'It's a family tradition to buy junk food for our road trips. Maybe not the best or healthiest tradition, but it's a treat, so choose something for you, and for Ella if there's something she can have.'

For a change from his usual savoury fare, Dan had a big tin of chewy-centred fruit-flavoured candies in his hand. Jess got mini ice-cream cones filled with marshmallow and topped with sprinkles for her baby daughter. 'Ella can go for an hour making a mess with one of those. Can I share your tin of candies, Dan?'

'Of course we can share.' He still had Ella in his arms, and his voice was deep. He looked tired and ruffled and as though he *still* hadn't had enough sleep.

Dan looked that way too often. Jess had been working hard to help him, but he was an automaton about getting through his work and everything going on with that firm in Sydney, about his children and stuff around the home as well. Jess suspected he'd been nothing but an automaton for a while now.

'I'll help you with them a lot, Dan. I'll make sure you get as much chance to rest over the next two days as is humanly possible.'

'You're generous, Jess. I —'

'Come on, Dad.' Rob bounced up and down on the balls of his feet. 'We're ready.'

'Jess, what sort of bathers do you have?' Mary came out of her shell to ask this, and to volunteer, 'Mine have pink, yellow and blue spots on them and they're really pretty. Annapolly has my old pair that I grew out of but she doesn't mind.'

'Um, well, I have a bikini.' Jess glanced at the several interested heads that had turned their way as this question was asked. Local women, doing their grocery shopping in the store, and already looking at Jess and Dan.

Jess didn't want to look at Dan, or to remember buying the bikini as her treat to herself after she got her figure back from having Ella. At the time, when she saw it on the sale rack and in her post-baby induced state, it had seemed like a good idea.

And then Jess had worn it carefully at home, in the secluded part of the backyard when she had Ella in the baby wader pool she'd also bought very cheaply. She had never let anyone else see her in it.

Well, it wasn't her fault if her curvy bits were a bit curvier these days than they had been. She coughed. 'I, um, I don't go swimming much.'

'What's it look like? What colour is it?' Mary asked the questions so innocently and she waited very earnestly for Jess to explain.

'Well, it's bright yellow with, um, with bumblebees on it. There are two parts to it and I usually wear a sarong over it. Do you know what a sarong is?' Jess wasn't about to miss the chance to interact with Dan's shyest child, but she would far rather describe a sarong than her bathers in any more detail.

She told herself Dan wasn't there with his ears on fire, and her bathers weren't that exciting.

She didn't mean *that* kind of exciting in any case.

Oh, Jess didn't know what the heck she meant and she'd been fine until it seemed as though the entire supermarket waited with bated breath for her answers about her swimming attire. Jess quickly explained about the sarong.

'Let's get these things bought so we can get back in the van.' She herded everyone to the checkout area. 'The sooner we get moving, the sooner we'll arrive at the beach.'

'Mary didn't mean any harm with her questions.' Dan spoke the words quietly into her ear as his children surged ahead to swarm into the van with their now purchased, and therefore consumable, goodies. A grin teased up one side of his mouth. 'And I'm sure you'll look lovely in yellow and bumblebees.'

He was in holiday mode. Dan's teasing was nothing but that, Jess assured herself. She tried very hard to believe it because she shouldn't hope for anything else.

She *didn't* hope for anything else. Did she?

'I know Mary was only curious.' Despite herself, Jess wondered if Dan *had* just flirted with her? Or simply teased her? Jess's gaze made its way inexorably to his face and discovered . . . he had done both! Well, that wasn't supposed to make Jess's heart feel all warm and mushy right along with a kick into overdrive of her pulse rate, but Dan was really attracted to her? Truly?

And why would that make you happy, Jess? It's bad enough that you've been noticing him. Do you really want to start thinking along those lines when you know how much your trust got shattered the last time you let yourself care for a man?

There were a dozen reasons why it would be smarter if Jess *didn't* care for this man!

Dan started the trip with some rock music. His children groaned but he ignored them. He had to have an occasional vice.

When he turned the music down twenty minutes later Jess glanced his way and gave a soft laugh. 'On the bright side, you're educating them by playing that song list.'

'How did you know I've used that justification?' He glanced at her, just once.

Her eyes were such a soft grey that it might be just as well he needed to concentrate on the road because the alternative was to get lost in those gentle depths. Those eyes were letting him in perhaps more than she realised right now.

Was he starting to care too much about Jessica Baker? He'd pushed this trip into being for his children, but he'd done it for Jess and Ella, too. He'd wanted them to be part of it, not simply because a second adult would be a good idea. Dan had wanted to do something for Jess that she might enjoy, give her something she might not otherwise have.

He wanted to see the worry disappear from the backs of her eyes, Dan realised. To see her completely relax even if only for a

little while, as he managed to relax sometimes.

When was the last time you did that?

Dan could relax with Jess.

Again the thought crept up on him.

It was the last thing that should be in his
mind because why on earth would Jess want
that? She was young and vibrant — young
enough that like his children she probably
thought his rock music was a piece of
ancient history. It was disloyal to the
memory of Rebecca anyway and Dan . . .
still loved her?

Well, how did he answer that question? Of
course he'd loved Rebecca. But he had also
grieved for her and got over losing her
because he had had no choice.

'Are we there yet?' Annapolly asked the
question.

'No, Annapolly, we're not there yet.' Dan
turned his attention to getting his family to
their seaside destination.

And turned his thoughts away from the
woman seated beside him in the front of
the van. Away from noticing the way the air
conditioning ruffled wisps of hair against
her cheek. From the smell of a light, floral
perfume blended with her skin.

Dan was not to be conscious of anything
other than his responsibilities as a father

and a family man and that was all. He wasn't avoiding dealing with any issues. He was simply being practical.

'That was a good kick, Rob. Well done.' Jess watched Dan's second eldest run up the beach to retrieve the soccer ball.

It was just after seven in the evening. There was a smattering of people on the beach, and a number of Fraziers all enjoying their visit to the seaside. Jess had to admit she was excited, too, if determined to keep very good watch over her crowd of charges.

The day had been beautiful and now they had a blue sky waning towards dusk, a soft, cooling sea breeze and the sun warm but not so baking hot that it would spoil their fun. There were miles of soft sandy beach with a ridge of shells tossed higher up. That augured well for collecting more of the same tomorrow morning. And the water itself. Oh, those rolling waves of endless blue water.

Jess let her gaze scan the scene again. Ella sat on a very large beach blanket beneath one of the umbrellas. She was quite content playing with a set of buckets that fitted inside each other and a plastic spade, which she banged on the buckets, chuckling gleefully as she did so.

Luke was in the water and his father was out there with him keeping a close eye, though the teen was a strong swimmer and a sensible one so far. Rob had taken his dip and got out to run up and down the beach. Mary and Annapolly had been given turns 'swimming' in the shallows with their dad before they came out to build a sandcastle.

Jess hadn't swum. Of course she'd love to, but she had a job to do. She was relieved that she wouldn't have to reveal the bumble-bee bikini hidden away nicely beneath her sarong.

Dan was a good swimmer, too, though Jess had tried not to look too closely at him once he stripped off his shirt and the cut-offs and revealed a pair of board shorts.

'It's your turn to have a swim, Jess. Luke and I are going to take a rest. I'll watch Ella while you're in there.' Dan glanced at Ella in time to see her bang the spade on one of the buckets again and crow in delight at the resulting 'thwack' of sound. 'She seems content enough.'

Droplets of water trickled from Dan's wet hair, and down the tanned muscles of his chest. His board shorts clung to his physique —

Well, Jess didn't need to be thinking about

Dan's physique!

Dan's gaze came back to her. An edge of intensity appeared in his eyes that suggested he might have noticed her examination of him, or might be making one of his own across Jess's sun-kissed shoulders and down over her arms.

Dan's shoulders and upper arms were strong, the muscles defined and beautifully curved.

Looking away now.

And his tummy was really flat. And he was tanned and strong and, oh, she really wanted to touch all that wet, salty skin with her fingertips.

'I don't think I'll swim.' *I'd probably set the sea on fire from all the heat that just rushed into me thanks to those thoughts.* Not to mention the bumblebees and all the curves that were more curves than they used to be. 'I, well, I probably just won't.'

She didn't want to strip down to her bikini in front of — the children? Jess glanced down at her bright, multicoloured sarong, and then, despite herself, looked a little longingly at the water, and along the beach to where there were several women wearing bikinis far more revealing than her very ordinary one, even if it was bright and covered in bees.

'This trip . . .' Dan hesitated. 'I wanted to do something for the children, *and* for you and Ella. It's not much of a trip to the beach if you don't swim. I won't laugh at the bumblebees, I promise.'

Oh, that serious tone with the glints of mischief dancing in his eyes, all because Mary had asked those questions in the supermarket and Dan had been right there while Jess squirmed her way through the answers.

Luke had moved away, and Jess felt for a moment as though she and Dan were the only people on the beach, despite the children surrounding them.

Dan probably wouldn't even look at her anyway. He just wanted her to be able to enjoy herself, and she was being ridiculous.

'I'm a decent swimmer.' Jess made the decision that she would get in the water. If Dan could stand here dripping in board shorts, Jess could strip down to curvy bumblebees. 'I'll make sure I do the right thing out there. You'll have to watch all the children while I'm gone.'

As though Dan weren't more than aware of the necessity of keeping charge of his children. And Ella, of course. It went without saying. He'd just offered to do exactly that.

Jess was procrastinating. 'Right.' She dumped the sarong in one swift movement. She did not boggle at the thought of the bumblebees on her butt. She *certainly* didn't have that very old song about being afraid to get in the water flash through her brain.

If she didn't meet Dan's eyes then she wouldn't even know if he was looking or not.

'You have a perfect figure.' He said it in a half whisper. 'I suppose I knew, really, but I couldn't have imagined.' The words ended. Dan's hot gaze had travelled over her and Jess had seen it. He turned abruptly away and Jess tried to walk very naturally across the sand to the water.

She swam and pushed her thoughts away until there was only swimming and the tug of the waves, and Dan and the children on the beach.

Dan hadn't really given her that intense look, she assured herself, forgetting that she wasn't thinking while she was out here.

Sure. Just as you didn't give Dan *an intense look.*

Jess forced her arms and legs to work for her, and rode the gentle waves, imagined bobbing like a cork. She kept the shore in her sights, but she let everything blur around the edges and she was successful eventually.

'Daddy, can I have a s'rong like Jess's? And why don't me and Daisy and Annapolly have 'kinis?' The question came from Mary as she sat down beside Dan where he'd come to play with Ella on her blanket.

Jess's daughter had noticed her mother's absence, but there were enough Fraziers to keep her distracted.

Dan was distracted. Mightily. The memory of Jess whipping off that sarong and dumping the colourful fabric onto the sand played through his mind over and over.

Not because of the sarong, but because of what it had revealed. Dan had never seen bumblebees look quite like that.

Jess was beautiful, curvy in all the right places, soft enough that he could imagine how nice it would feel to cuddle her —

'Dad?' Mary poked him in the ribs with one finger. 'Did you hear me?'

'You and your sisters have those bathing suits because they look good on you.' Dan dragged his gaze away from the sight of Jess out there enjoying her time in the water.

His voice dropped about an octave as he went on. 'Jess has her suit because it looks good on her, too.'

'She shouldn't dress like that when she's

supposed to be working for us, looking after everyone.' Luke's words came from behind Dan with low anger. 'She's just trying to make you interested in her, and all you do is look at her all the time. I hate her and I wish you'd never hired her!'

'What's got into you, Luke?' Dan turned and stared into his son's set, angry face.

Luke's glance shifted beyond him. 'I mean every word of it and don't tell me to apologise, Dad, because I won't. On top of everything, you're treating her like she's part of the family. She's not. She's just the babysitter and not even a good one because she let Annapolly hurt herself.'

'Apologise, Luke.' Dan started to his feet.

Luke was faster. He shook his head and stalked away across the beach.

Dan didn't need to turn to know that Jess was standing there, but he looked anyway, and caught her determined, forced smile as she reached for her sarong and pulled it over the bumblebees. 'Don't force him, Dan. He won't mean it anyway, if you do that.'

Had Dan allowed the sight of her to short-circuit his sensible brain functions?

And Jess's eyes had clouded over with desire when she'd seen his bare chest . . . How did he feel about that?

Should he only worry about Luke's behaviour and ignore the rest of this? Dan was usually controlled and focused. Right now he didn't know which urge to cater to first. He wanted to chase after Luke and demand an explanation and apology, which would no doubt end in an argument because right now his son wasn't in the frame of mind to be reasonable and Dan didn't exactly feel like being tolerant either.

Or should he try to sort this out with Jess? 'I can't allow him to speak that way.'

'No, but you can give him time to cool off a bit just now.' Jess stuck her chin out. 'Thanks, anyway, for the swim, and if you think I've dressed inappropriately —'

'I don't think that.' Dan frowned. 'And Luke was having a go at me as much as at you.' As each word emerged Dan wanted to become angrier, and he battled to push back the feeling. Something told him once he asked himself just *why* he felt so resentful of Luke's attitude, he would have to deal with a whole bunch of questions he wasn't sure he was ready to confront.

'Well, it was nice to swim. I haven't had a swim in the sea for years.' Jess drew a deep breath and seemed to come to a decision. 'If you feel it would be best to replace me, Dan, with someone Luke can get along better with —'

'That won't be necessary.' Dan appreciated her making the offer, but he wasn't going to let her go. 'I don't want to lose you,
Jess.'

To lose her help, he'd meant.

But was that all he'd meant?

Dan glanced her way. Luke's outburst
notwithstanding, Dan *was* becoming more
and more attracted to Jess. Even in the face
of the conflict with Luke, Dan wanted to
get to the end of the day and all the children
in bed. And why did he want that?

So he could find a private nook and kiss
Jess stupid? Dan acknowledged he would
like to do exactly that. Did he really think it
would resolve anything? It would just com-
plicate things even more.

'I'm glad you enjoyed the water.' He felt
not quite certain of his ground. When Dan
worked he *was* completely certain of his
ground. He was good at his job and he did
it well, and he powered through it with a
great deal of focus while he still managed to
watch the children besides. Yet right now
Dan felt as though there were other parts of
him that hadn't been living.

He shouldn't be feeling like this. In the
end he'd made the choice to be content, so
why did Luke's attitude bother him so
much? Because there was something more

to it than Luke needing to mind his manners around Jess, though that was very important.

'I think we'd better pack up and head back to the beach house.' Dan got to his feet and started gathering paraphernalia together. Perhaps once there, all of these feelings would settle down.

He felt weird when he lifted the beach umbrella out of the sand. Dan brushed the feeling aside and got on with rounding up the children. They'd go back to the beach house, maybe buy fish and chips on the way from a local shop, eat, and he expected the children would fall asleep quite quickly because it *had* been a long day. The thought of a nice salty meal of fresh seafood did appeal. It might halfway reward him for the talk he was going to have to have with his son.

'Mum used to make great sandcastles when we went to the beach.' Rob's words were directed to Jess.

Luke had yet again stalked ahead of the family to the van.

'What sort of castles do you remember, Rob?' Jess ruffled the boy's hair before she bent to pick up her daughter from the blanket.

It was the first time Dan had heard any of

his children mention Rebecca to their care-giver. But that wasn't the reason the words sliced right through Dan.

He hadn't thought once about Rebecca while they were at the beach. For the first day since he lost her, Dan hadn't had a thought in his head about the mother of his children. All those thoughts had been directed at Jess, to being so conscious of her.

Luke's anger had been towards Jess, and Dan, but had it really been about this? Had Luke somehow seen that his father was drifting from those memories and Luke felt resentful and lost as a result? Dan felt lost as he asked this question because he didn't know. He hadn't wanted to forget. He couldn't forget.

Rob started to explain the intricate sand-castles he remembered building with his mother. Dan added his few words here and there because the children would have felt it was strange if he didn't. He got everyone packed into the van. And guilt ate at him because his heart had been given to Rebecca and there was nothing left, so why did he think it was okay to want Jessica Baker?

To think about things with her that had been part of his marriage? Not only physi-cal closeness, but friendship and getting to know a woman and wanting to be part of *her* life, to understand her better.

Dan set the van in motion.

He had no answers. All he had were questions that he didn't want to know about and a son he had to deal with when he got him to himself for a moment!

CHAPTER SEVEN

'They're all down for the count finally.' Jess made the announcement as she joined Dan on the front porch of the compact beach house. It was almost midnight. The younger children had been overtired and excitable.

Dan had taken Luke away in the van straight after dinner and they'd both come back looking like thunderclouds. Actually Luke had seemed on the verge of tears, a fact Jess had noted and made sure she drew the attention of the other children away from him, and kept it away. She didn't want him to feel the sting of embarrassment. Her heart ached for the boy and she wished she could find some way to help him, or at least help him to know that she meant him no harm.

And yet her feelings towards Dan hadn't changed. Jess couldn't shut them down because of Luke. They were there. Tonight Jess needed to comfort Dan, and be comforted by him, as much as she needed to try to reach out to his son. This tangle of feelings wasn't easy.

'Thanks, Jess. It was a busy and long enough day.' Dan was seated on the only piece of furniture out here, which happened to be a swing seat. He bent down and retrieved two glasses of white wine from the floor beside it, and held one out to her.

Jess sat, and took the wine from him with a surprised and grateful sigh. 'Where did you find this?'

'It was in the fridge, part of the service for renting this seaside cottage.' Dan smiled. 'Tonight I think we've both earned a glass.'

'I won't argue.' Jess sipped the wine and closed her eyes and let the fruity tang of it slide across her tongue.

Dan set the swing into gentle motion, and she leaned back and let the sound of the ocean, the sea breeze, the taste of the wine all touch her senses.

And Dan, Jess? Is he touching your senses too?

Oh, she was super aware of him seated beside her. Their thighs were almost brushing. Dan had his wineglass in one hand. His other arm was draped across the back of the seat. If she leaned back a little more she would practically *be* in his arms.

Jess wanted to be, that was the trouble. She wanted to be in Dan's embrace more than anything and she couldn't let herself want that. There were so many reasons. She was Dan's employee. Her home was under threat. She needed her job with Dan for as long as he wanted to keep her on, to get money to pay off the debt on her cottage. Dan had only just spoken to Luke to try to get him into a better place about Jess's presence as the caregiver. Jess was younger. Dan was older. He was her employer.

There were other reasons why Jess couldn't trust —

'I hope today didn't exhaust you too much, Jess.' Dan's low words came to her through the quiet of the night.

Came on a breath and she turned her head. Light spilled from the lounge room inside. She'd walked out through the sliding doors to join Dan on the porch. The light illuminated just enough for Jess to see the strong planes of Dan's face and to want to trace each one of them with her fingertips.

Her worries blurred as she stared into his eyes. Her sensible reasons for resisting the way he made her feel faded too.

'It didn't exhaust me. But what about you, Dan? I don't think you managed much rest for yourself today.' In fact, Jess thought Dan might have overdone it a bit today, because he'd looked quite used up when they left the beach, and again after playing in the yard with Rob for a while tonight.

He'd looked upset, too, when Rob mentioned building sandcastles with . . . Rebecca, Dan's late wife. She'd been a beautiful brunette with soft brown eyes and a smile that Dan must see in his daughters every day. Jess had pored over the framed photos with the younger children back at the Fraziers' house.

And the talk with Luke couldn't have been easy for Dan, either.

'A good sleep tonight will sort me out.' Dan shifted slightly, slowed the movement of the swing seat down to the gentlest motion. As he did so his thigh shifted against Jess's. She had a skirt on with a T-shirt top. Dan was wearing another of his polo shirts and denim shorts. Yet even through the layers of skirt and shorts, Jess's skin warmed, sensitised to that brush of his body against her.

'What do you have planned for the kids tomorrow — ?'

'I hope the children don't wake at dawn tomorrow —'

Jess drew a tight breath.

Dan stopped.

Their eyes met and held, and Dan made a sound that was half yielding, half resistant, and Jess's breath stopped in her throat.

'Jess.' Dan spoke her name with all the suppressed desire that Jess felt.

She should say no, should get up, walk away, think about her position here and all those reasons, but Jess didn't. She couldn't do it because she did desire Dan. She was attracted to him and in the back of her mind she had asked herself a hundred times —

When Dan lowered his head, she lifted her lips and met him. His foot came to rest on the floor and the tiny motion of the swing seat stopped.

Dan's lips closed over Jess's and his arms came around her. Her arms rose to his chest and one locked about the back of his neck. Jess had dreamed about Dan's neck. The strong column of it; how the muscles would feel beneath her hand. She hadn't known that he would feel so warm. That she would feel such tensile strength in him, or that his kiss would feel like this. She told herself it was safe. The children were asleep. She and Dan could do this and it wasn't hurting anything.

Dan's firm lips softened, and brought her the taste of wine that was also in her mouth. Jess's wineglass was long gone, somewhere on the floor. She didn't even remember finishing the drink or putting it down. She wanted to blame the abandonment of her thoughts on that wine but she couldn't.

The bubbles floating inside her were not from the small amount of alcohol. These were Dan-inspired bubbles and Jess didn't want them to ever stop. All her careful thoughts and self-protection frayed away, unravelled as Dan's lips consumed hers, took her mouth with desire and a need that matched her need.

Jess melted into him. That was what Dan felt as he kissed her, as their lips meshed together and he experienced all the sensations of holding her, kissing her, feeling her body soften against his and her arm creep about his neck so she could hold him closer, draw more from their kiss.

His heart pounded. Every sense and sensation was focused on the woman in his arms, the taste of her soft lips. Dan had asked himself how Jess could truly be attracted to him, what she could see in a man his age. There was Luke, being difficult, and Dan's own confused feelings.

And there was this — him kissing her and her kissing him in a way that not only assuaged curiosity and awareness but invoked tenderness, the kind of tenderness he would

have given and exchanged only with Rebecca . . .

What was he doing?

What kind of risk was he taking when he
had nothing inside him to give, nothing that
hadn't already been given, handed over to
the woman he had loved with all his heart?
What was he doing seeking this with Jess
when his eldest son was inside, angry and
upset because he thought Dan was crossing
a line with an employee that he shouldn't
cross?

Luke had thrown that at Dan along with a
lot of deeper accusations about Dan not ho-
nouring his mother, and Dan . . . hadn't
been able to argue because Luke was right
about Jess's position as an employee, and in
the end, though Dan didn't want his son
trying to dictate to him about his personal
life, Luke's accusations about the rest of it
only matched Dan's own thoughts too.

Dan's hands came up to Jess's shoulders.
He eased his lips from hers and set distance
between them. Dan on this side of the swing
seat. Jess on that side. And he prayed to
whatever god might be listening that he
hadn't just hurt her and that he hadn't just
hurt himself. This *wasn't* right.

It couldn't be.

Regret washed through him. For doing

something that was wrong and disloyal. He couldn't remember how it had felt to kiss Rebecca. The memory wouldn't come, was pushed down beneath the sensation of kissing his children's daycare mum. Dan had always been able to remember.

Yet this kiss had felt special, exceptional, but was he talking himself into these thoughts because he craved closeness? Because Jess was attractive and working in proximity with him and so it was almost easy to let himself — ?

'It's the holiday setting.' A trace of panic laced Jess's tone. She blinked as though to try to dispel the lingering effects of what they had just shared. 'The sea and how late it is and sitting out here. It didn't mean anything. We just didn't think —'

But they had thought, hadn't they? Dan had known that Jess would join him out here and he'd waited and in some part of him he'd known he would kiss her, even despite the upheaval with his son and all the reasons it would have been smarter not to do it.

Jess had done her final round inside the house and checked on her daughter and she'd known, too. Dan felt certain that she had. But could she be more truly invested in this than he was?

Jess was young, a single mother and working for him. Why put her in a position where she might feel vulnerable, whether she'd been prepared to step into that place with him for a moment or not?

She was obviously having second thoughts about it now.

Just as he was. 'I had no right to do that, Jess, and yet a part of me wanted it to happen.' He hated to admit it but he couldn't make it sound as though Jess had been the one to try to make it happen. They'd both drifted towards this and in the quiet of the night with all the children tucked away . . . 'That was even more wrong because I know I can't —'

'I know.' Jess hushed him with the low words. 'I know, Dan.' She got up from the seat. Her face was tight, filled with tense emotion. Uncertainty and resolve at war with each other. Shadows. Unease. And still the impact of his kisses was there for him to see upon her swollen lips and in the blurred confusion in her soft grey eyes.

Desire whispered again, and Dan frowned it down.

'It's late.' The need to get away filled her words. 'And I think the children probably will be up early in the morning. I need to be up too, to be on duty the moment they wake and to do my best to start trying to win Luke's trust again after — after him opening up about his feelings today.'

She didn't say more and Dan pushed down his own mixed feelings on that topic for examination later.

Jess simply went on. 'So I'll say goodnight now and hope that you sleep well and get really good rest. I worry about you getting too tired sometimes.'

She went inside. Dan picked up the wineglasses, and dumped them in the kitchen, and made sure all the doors were locked. He would do as Jess suggested and sleep, and when he woke tomorrow he'd remember what it had been like to kiss Rebecca.

There would be no Dan and Jess, because Dan and Jess didn't exist. Not in any way other than employer and employee. He might be tempted, he might need to draw some lines in the sand with his son so Luke respected Dan's right to have needs, but none of that changed the fact that his relationship with his much younger childcare provider needed to remain firmly fixed in business.

Dan took himself off to bed.

Jess leaned against the closed door of the room she was sharing with Ella. She'd shut herself in there and listened as Dan went about the house checking that everything was locked up and secure. Checking that his children, and, by association because they were here, Jess and Ella, were safe before he went to bed.

Dan had kissed her. Jess's insides were still shaking from the impact of that kiss. She didn't want to think about it, was afraid if she did she might discover thoughts and reactions and emotions inside herself she couldn't let herself find.

He'd pushed her away, had regretted the kiss probably before it was even over. Jess had seen in Dan's eyes the conviction that she would be too much trouble to be worth it. Some of that would be about Luke's attitude, about her working for him . . .

People found ways, though, when things mattered enough, didn't they?

You don't want *Dan to find a way, Jess.*

Jess didn't have what she would need to invest emotionally. She had her life to live and she needed to rely on herself, be the best mother possible to Ella and the best daycare mum she could be, but with the exception of the love she gave to her daughter, Jess needed to do those things while keeping the deepest parts of herself locked away where they would stay safe and not suffer any further blows of rejection.

What could Dan Frazier do but reject Jess? He'd done it just now, hadn't he?

Jess pushed away from the door and went to the single bed beside her daughter's cot. Jess's clothes were there in a zipper bag. She got out her pyjamas, put them on, crawled under the sheet and prayed for sleep and for tomorrow to have erased every memory of Dan's mouth over hers, his arms snug about her, and most of all to have erased the feeling of security and rightness that Jess had felt in his embrace.

There was no such security to be found. Dan didn't have it to give.

'Eating outside at a picnic table is fun. I'm glad we thought of it.' Daisy didn't hesitate to take credit for the idea of eating their breakfast out of doors, though in fact it had been Dan's suggestion because he'd wanted to allow Jess to sleep in a little if she could.

It was not because he didn't feel ready to face her after that kiss. Dan glanced in Luke's direction. Was it because of the uneasy state of matters between him and his son? It was, in part. It was also because Dan hadn't been able to get the kiss out of his mind.

'Do we have any more orange juice, Dad?'

Rob asked the question after lifting the two-litre bottle on the table and discovering it was empty.

'You keep going on your breakfast, Rob. I'll get more juice from the fridge.' Dan left the children. It was bad that, because of Luke, he almost felt relieved to walk away. He was going to have to try to sort things out better than this, but what should he say? Butt out of my personal life? It's none of your business? It wasn't that simple.

Dan stepped into the kitchen, and heard a sound from the room Jess and Ella were sharing. The door had been closed when he got up this morning but he noted now that it was halfway open.

Had Annapolly taken a peek in there? She was a horror for helping herself to doors that weren't locked. Dan hesitated for a moment and then decided to go shut it. It was six in the morning. Let Jess sleep in while she could. Ella, too.

Let a little more time pass before Dan had to confront what happened last night? The awareness *was* mostly due to proximity, wasn't it? And to his senses waking up after a four-year slumber in a way Dan hadn't realised was going to sneak up on him?

He stepped quietly to the door of the room and reached to pull it closed.

He paused as he took in the sight inside. A baby in a cot, covers kicked off lying on her tummy with her nappy-padded bum in the air. A smile twitched at the corners of Dan's mouth despite himself.

Then his gaze shifted to the bed beside that cot and his smile faded because there was Jess in a set of very short floral baby-doll pyjamas with frilly bits all over and a lot of bare skin. She, too, had kicked off her covers and was sound asleep on her tummy.

And yes, Dan was still attracted and it had only taken that glimpse of her to make it clear. But there was more than that. There was tightness in Dan's chest because . . . he wanted to step into the room, climb into the bed, pull the sheet up over both of them and cuddle up with her. He wanted that, and it wasn't only about physical awareness. It was about a kind of closeness that Dan feared might mean he didn't only *want* her, but some part of him thought that he needed her?

'Du!' A wriggle of sound came from the cot.

By the time Dan looked, Ella was on her back, grinning up at him.

'Do you want to get up, Ella?' Dan whispered and shifted to the side of the cot. The little one wriggled, rolled and pulled herself up to her feet using the cot's railings for support.

Dan picked her up, grabbed a disposable nappy and the bits and pieces he'd need to sort her out, and took her into the girls' room. Two minutes later he had a dry cooing baby in his arms. He got Rob's juice from the fridge and took Ella outside to join the others.

The children fussed over Ella. She was a beautiful baby. Dan had forgotten what it was like to have such a little one. Ella was wide awake but still a bit cuddly. She laid her head in the crook of his neck and watched his rowdy family from the safety of his arms. And Dan . . . wished that all of life could be so simple. Just provide a pair of arms and that would be enough.

Luke had the seat to Dan's right. Ella reached out her arms to him and gurgled.

'I think she wants you to hold her, Luke.' Dan caught his son's eye just as Ella wiggled even more, waving her arms for Luke to take her.

'I don't know why she likes me so much.' Luke half grumbled the words, but he took Ella and his expression was soft as he sat her on his knees.

Dan looked at his eldest, who was so close to being a man now, and wondered where the years had gone, and hoped that he and Luke wouldn't remain at loggerheads. He didn't want that. Deep down, Dan didn't think Luke wanted that, either.

And Dan thought about Jess asleep in bed inside and how he'd felt when he saw her there. Maybe what he felt was lonely, and Jess was around and he'd kissed her so of course he'd want to kiss her again . . .

Dan poured himself some cereal, added a generous portion of milk, and started a conversation with the children about what they'd be doing today before they got in the van to go back home.

Probably when Jess woke, Dan would look at her and wonder what all his fuss had been about anyway.

'You let me sleep in.' Jess spoke the words in a shocked tone as she joined Dan at the outdoor breakfast table. She'd woken to the sound of Ella crowing somewhere outside and had realised Dan must have got her daughter up and left Jess to sleep.

Jess had never started a day without taking care of Ella. And the thought of Dan coming into the room, seeing her sleeping . . .

What if she'd been flat on her back snoring? She'd woken on her side, curled up in a ball, but Jess knew she wriggled around before she actually woke up. Ella did the same thing.

'You're dressed.' Dan spoke the words with an edge of relief. A second later his ears turned red at the tips. He glanced at his children, then turned back to Jess and all but shoved a box of breakfast cereal her way as she took a seat at the table. 'You were asleep. I went to shut the door. I think Annapolly was the culprit though I couldn't say for sure. Ella was awake but I couldn't see the sense in waking you.'

With these statements made, Dan poured a glass of juice for himself and drank half of it in one gulp.

There hadn't been time from waking to joining everyone at the table for Jess to think about anything other than the shock of waking without her daughter in the room, and knowing she should be on duty and Dan had left her to sleep. She'd thrown on the first clothes she found and rushed outside. She hadn't even combed her hair, and now Jess became aware of so many things all at once.

Her less-than-properly-groomed state. Dan looking fresh and attractive and far more capable of satisfying her than any bowl of cereal.

Luke holding her daughter, and Ella patting his face with complete contentment. Jess had a theory about that. Children and animals — they knew a kind heart when they found one. That gave Jess hope that she *would* be able to get things in a better place with Luke over time.

If you stop showing any interest in his father!

Jess had realised that kissing Dan had been a mistake. All she'd done was expose herself to Dan backing away afterwards. But this morning Jess was having trouble accepting that assessment. What was wrong with her? Did she want to line up to be rejected when she couldn't stack up to what Dan had already had in his life? When Dan wasn't prepared to stand up for her? Not really? If he cared enough he would address the issue with his son and make it clear to Luke that he had the right to pursue a relationship.

Hadn't she had enough second-rate treatment from Ella's father?

Jess didn't want to be negative. She had Ella. She had a job and she would have a home. Jess just needed to sort that out properly with Lang Fielder one day very soon. She didn't need anything more.

Jess pushed out every thought aside from her work, this work right now. And she worked. She made sure the children had the best time possible when they all went back to the beach. She gave two hundred per cent to trying to win Luke over. She assisted Dan at every turn and she did it without responding to him as a man, at all.

This was the way it needed to be. Jess and Dan, working as a team to give his children the best short holiday experience possible, and for Jess to give the best care for them, overall.

Jess reminded herself of these thoughts as the family made their way back to Dan's sprawling home late that day after touring two museums on the way home, and stopping for various adventures including afternoon tea at a truck stop.

'You can go, Jess. You must be as exhausted as I am.' Dan seemed to have to dig for the smile he offered.

'Thanks for taking me and Ella along for the trip.' Jess made a point of saying goodnight to each of the children before she lifted her sleeping daughter into her arms.

It didn't matter if Luke didn't respond. He *was* softening. Jess could sense it.

And you don't think that's simply because he told his father to stay away from you and he's getting the impression Dan obeyed?

What a tangle it was!

Dan brought her luggage to the car for her, and Jess finished her thanks loudly enough that if any of the children were inclined, they would hear every word. 'It was a treat I doubt I'd have been able to give Ella any time soon and I appreciate it for that reason.'

'And I appreciated having help while we were there.' Dan's eyes were cloudy with a combination of exhaustion and banked-down longing when Jess straightened from strapping Ella into her car restraint.

A moment later he blinked and that impression was gone. Had Jess imagined it? Or was Dan still struggling, after all, to set aside those feelings?

Oh, Jess, don't hope for that to be the case! Jess couldn't let herself think about consciousness. *Dan* didn't want to think about it. Dan . . . didn't want Jess. This was clear, and Jess needed to keep it clear within herself. 'Goodnight, Dan. I'll be here day after tomorrow as usual.' She would be here for as long as he could offer her work.

And in the end that was that, wasn't it? Jess needed to keep trying to find other, ongoing work, too, and most of all she needed to forget all about any feelings towards this man who was a temporary employer and nothing else.

CHAPTER EIGHT

'Jess.' Dan's deep voice said her name with concern. A moment later he had hold of her shoulder. 'What's wrong?'

'I'm fine, Dan. There's nothing wrong.' Jess blinked furiously and forced a smile, determined to make Dan believe it.

Dan had come upon her in the hallway outside the room that held Ella's travel cot. Her grumpy baby had finally given in to sleep after being fractious all morning. Had Dan noticed that Jess had been struggling to do her job properly with the rest of the children because of Ella's mood?

If Ella's in a mood, it's more than likely because she's picked up on her mother's anxiety.

'I'm sorry, Dan. I hope Ella's grizzling didn't disturb your work in the den.' When Ella had finally given in and fallen asleep, Jess hadn't been able to hold back that anxiety any longer. She'd leaned against the wall outside Ella's room and panic had washed over her. She hadn't expected Dan to come along and find her there.

'If she's sick or you need anything —' Dan didn't seem to be aware that his fingers were gently rubbing at Jess's shoulders.

Jess wanted to lean her head forward onto his chest, take what comfort she could. For a split second she even considered pretending that Ella's grizzling had been anything more than reacting to Jess's mood, but it hadn't been. 'Ella's fine. She'll sleep now and have forgotten her grumpiness when she wakes.'

'Okay. If you're sure.' Dan dropped his hands but his gaze didn't leave her face.

'I need to check on the girls, Dan.' Jess didn't. Not really. They were content playing tea parties on the veranda. Dan's sons were riding their pushbikes around the front part of the ten-acre allotment, where Jess could still look out periodically and keep an eye on them.

If anything, at the moment, Luke seemed to be cold towards his father rather than Jess. Not that there was a whole lot of comfort in that.

'The girls are happy enough. I can see Rob and Luke out there on their bikes and they're fine for the moment, too.' Dan blew out a breath. 'There's something troubling you, enough that you looked devastated just now. I'm sorry if I caught you while your guard was down, but I wish you'd tell me, Jess. If it was Luke —'

'No, Luke had his say at the beach. I'm sure if you feel there's a need to encourage Luke to change his attitude about your personal life, you'll address that topic with him.' Did Jess sound snippy saying that?

You have a right to your opinion about it. Dan made it pretty clear he wasn't prepared to go into battle with his son over any involvement he might want with you.

But that was just it. Dan *didn't* want to be involved with Jess. How many times would she have to remind herself of that fact before it truly sank in?

And Dan wasn't a horrid man. He was just one who had kissed her, and then decided that hadn't been a smart idea. Jess had agreed with him, so why was she going on about it now? She didn't *want* Dan and Luke to battle because of her.

'Jess.' Dan's voice softened again. 'I know there have been some tough patches. I've added to some of those for you and . . . I regret that. But won't you tell me what's wrong now?'

Jess looked into Dan's eyes and there was

139

something in there of the day *she* had asked *him* if she could help him. A fellow feeling, at least. A measure of care.

'I'm going to lose my home. Ella's father didn't turn out to be a very nice person.' Jess hadn't understood that until it was too late, and maybe she should have held back from admitting it to Dan, but he'd once said that he wanted to know more about her life.

This was a major part of her history, but Dan had said that to her as her employer, at the start, not . . . as anything else. 'He didn't want a baby, and he didn't want me. After I told him Ella was on the way, he wanted me to sign an agreement that I would never name him as her father or ask him for any support and that Ella and I would get out of his life and stay out.'

Jess had been hurt and she needed to remember that pain and be careful not to let it happen again.

Somewhere along the line with Dan, she'd lost some of her focus.

A frown formed between Dan's brows. He took her by the elbow then, and ushered them both into the kitchen where he turned her to face him. 'If he fathered your baby, Jess, he owed you support. Financial maintenance at the least, throughout Ella's childhood.'

'I know.' And Jess did know. And she knew that Dan would never have behaved as Peter Rosche had done. She wasn't trying to judge Dan by Peter's standards, or lack of them.

Jess just didn't want to get hurt any more. She pushed a sigh out between her lips. 'In theory, that's how it works but he'd made it so clear he didn't want anything to do with either of us. I thought he'd only be a horrid influence in Ella's life anyway.

'I signed his agreement and I thought I'd been smart because I bargained to have him buy the little cottage here for me so I'd have a safe place to raise Ella.'

Jess had pointed the cottage out to Dan when they came back from their trip to the beach, so he knew it was small, nothing special, though it was on a decent-sized block surrounded by three other cottage properties, all with an elevated view.

'What happened?'

'He bought the cottage and didn't tell me that he'd done a deal with the local council regarding ten years' worth of overdue rates on it.' Jess felt naive for letting that happen. 'Lang Fielder, the councillor, claims that he's been sending notices that the overdue rates and interest had to be paid, but those went to some address invented by Ella's father. It got to the point where Lang delivered a final notice to the property itself. That's when I found out about it.'

Dan nodded. 'That notice was delivered directly to you?'

'Yes. A couple of weeks ago.' Jess swallowed down on a mix of anxiety and frustration. She didn't want to let the anxiety win, but it really was getting the upper hand at the moment. 'The cottage isn't worth much, Dan. You've seen it. It's right on the edge of town. The shaded outdoor areas help for my daycare, but the cottage itself is quite small and very basic. Over one third of its value is owed to the council in back rates and accumulated interest. Ella's father has disappeared, and I've been given to the end of the month to pay all of it in full or they'll sell the property to get the money.'

The frown between Dan's eyes deepened. 'Have you spoken to a solicitor? You can't lose your home. That's not fair.'

No. It wasn't fair, but in Jess's experience not all of life always was. 'I got two letters in the mail yesterday while I was minding my other children. One was from the local solicitor I approached, to say they can't get legal aid funding to help me. I can't pay them normal rates, so that's the end of that. The other letter was from Lang Fielder at the council, formally declining my request to make ongoing payments off what's owed. He says because it's got as far as it has, the council is exercising its right to recoup the money by selling the property. Market value is irrelevant so long as it sells for enough to get their money back. And apparently the council already knows of an interested buyer.'

'I'll help you. There's got to be more —'

'It's not your responsibility, Dan.' Jess shook her head. She appreciated Dan's care, perhaps even more because it came purely from a temporary employer's perspective now.

That knowledge shouldn't have stung, but it did, a little.

Dan half turned away to get cups down and put on the kettle. He efficiently got tea making sorted before he faced her again. 'Jess, you got me out of a tight spot by offering to help me. I have a solicitor who's handled heaps of stuff for me. Let me ask him to look at your situation. If there's something that can be done, he'll be able to tell us.'

He held up a hand. 'And before you say anything about money, he won't charge me for this. He took over a smaller practice last year that had belonged to his uncle. The financials were in a mess and I sorted that out for him as a favour. He told me if I ever needed one back to let him know, so . . . let me call that favour in on your behalf.'

'You're not making that up to try to save my pride?' Because Jess simply wouldn't be able to tolerate that. Not at all. She searched his face.

He shook his head. 'It may not change anything, Jess, but you need to know where you stand legally. How about if I try to ring the guy now and you can speak with him and explain the situation?'

Dan took her silence as agreement, and made his way to the den. And that was fine because Jess needed help. She just hadn't expected to have it handed to her free of charge thanks to Dan's generosity, right when she was doing her best to feel resentful towards Dan for . . .

For what, Jessica? For not standing up to his son and pushing for the right to have a relationship with you, when you already knew deep down it would be dangerous to pursue such a relationship because you've been hurt before, and it would have been stupid to enter into anything like that when you work together as well?

Even with Luke's attitude aside, there were still plenty of valid reasons why Jess should have stayed away from letting herself desire Dan, and vice versa.

'Jess, I have the solicitor on the phone. His name is Jonathan Porerri.' Dan spoke from the doorway of his den. 'Just tell him what you told me. I've given him fax and email information and we've organised things so he's retained to assist you with this situation.'

Right. Jess's tummy knotted up, but she'd explained the situation to Dan. If that hadn't killed her she could explain it again to a stranger on the other end of a phone line. At least at the end of it she would come out with a better idea of where she stood, and therefore what her next movements needed to be, and how quickly she needed to make them. She had to take this opportunity to get some advice and be grateful for it.

Dan watched Jess step inside his den. He moved out of the room and closed the door behind him. How much trouble was she in? What kind of rat would treat her that way? Make her sign herself and her baby out of his life and in the process of doing that, set her up so he knew she wouldn't have a roof over her head a year later?

Instincts inside Dan were roaring. He wanted to find this man and make him take responsibility for his actions, for leaving Jess in a position where she was worrying about having a home.

Oh, yes? And you've treated her perfectly the entire time she's worked for you?

Dan hadn't, but that was complicated, and he certainly hadn't set out to harm Jess deliberately in any way. He would never try to do that.

'I've finished the call.' Jess stepped back into the kitchen several minutes later.

She was pale, but seemed very composed. *Too* composed? Dan opened his mouth to ask — he wasn't sure what.

But Jess met his gaze and spoke before he could. 'Thank you, Dan, for giving me the opportunity to pick your solicitor's brains about my situation. He's asked me to fax him some information that I need to get from the cottage. Would you mind if I collected that now? Ella's asleep.'

'Of course.' What Dan wanted most was to take her into his arms and comfort her. And that confused him. He believed, and he truly meant it, that it wasn't right to have any interest in Jess Baker aside from being her employer.

You're dodging issues, Dan. Luke's attitude is right up there with the best of those issues. Why do you think he feels so opposed to you

146

experiencing any interest in Jess? He believes you should only ever have feelings for his late mother, and . . .

What if Dan wanted to have feelings else-where?

Before he could think about that, Jess nodded and started for the door. 'I'll be back soon.'

Jess drove the short distance to her cottage. How much longer would she have it? Did she have to lose it? What work could she get to support her and Ella when all she knew was how to be a daycare mum?

Jess parked her little car beside her equally unpretentious cottage and forced a controlled expression to her face before she stepped out.

'Just get the paperwork. Ella's asleep back at Dan's. You don't have time to waste.' Jess got a small locked box and took out her copy of the agreement she'd signed with Peter Rosche and what paperwork he'd given her in relation to ownership of the cottage. There was nothing in it to say there were back rates owing, as Jess had checked at least ten times since Lang Fielder delivered that notice to her doorstep.

As she drove back towards Dan's house she passed Lang driving out towards her home looking smug. Well, if he'd been looking to speak with her he could just miss out. She'd rather hear back from this solicitor and then see what needed to be done.

'Oh, good, I can hear Ella starting to stir.' Jess spoke in the most determinedly cheerful tone she could muster as she stepped out of Dan's den ten minutes later. She'd faxed all the information to the solicitor and he'd told her he would speak with her by phone later in the day or tomorrow, to let her know his thoughts after reading everything. 'Thanks, Dan, for the use of your fax — and for the use of your solicitor.'

Jess started towards the room that held Ella's travel cot. 'Are we taking the children to the town fair? I know the boys were hoping they could go this afternoon.'

Once the words were out, Jess replayed them in her head and heat climbed into her cheeks because how could she just do that? Just assume it would be 'Jess and Dan' taking the children to the fair? As though they were all one big family and Jess had the right to make such sweeping suggestions.

No, she hadn't thought that, but Dan might be too busy. 'That is, *I* would be more than happy to take them.' And she would be, but there was another side to it. 'I'm just a bit concerned that it'll be like the

148

beach. I can imagine they'd have more fun if we didn't all have to stay together in one tight pack, but if I was on my own I wouldn't want them running rampant all over the fairground.' Not to mention if Luke decided to show his stubborn streak and go off on his own. 'But can you spare the time, Dan?'

'We'll all go. I'll make up the time later if I have to. We'll only be there a few hours.' Dan started towards the outside of the house. 'I'll go round up the boys. I suspect by the time I convince Rob he has to change into clean clothes before we leave, you'll have the girls sorted out.'

So they went to the town fair.

Jess came across the sons of a family she knew and introduced the boys to Rob and Luke. They got into conversation during the cow show.

'Actually those ones are bulls.' Jess said this to Mary, who'd made the observation that the cow part of the fair wasn't all that interesting.

'Why don't you come to our place one day soon?' One of the boys made this invitation to Luke and Rob. 'We've got heaps of cool computer games and other things.'

Rob's eyes lit up. 'Can we, Dad?'

'If the parents would like to give a call to

149

confirm it's okay, yes.'

Dan handed over a business card with his mobile number on it. They went their separate ways then.

Jess walked at Dan's side pushing Ella in the stroller, and refused to think about the picture of a family that they must all make. They weren't a family. They were two very separate families, but, more even than that, Jess was the employee. That put her in a whole different league.

'We're going on that one, Dad.' Rob pointed to a ride that gave Jess vertigo just trying to look at it. 'It's got to be the best one here.'

Jess took the girls to various sideshow stalls, and showed them through the big hall filled with craft items and baked goods before they went in search of Dan and his sons again.

'Dad, will you take me on that ride? Please? I want to go on it, but not by myself.' Mary asked the question of her father while Rob and Luke made their way forward in a queue for another more adventurous ride.

The ride Mary had indicated was a beginner's ride with completely enclosed cage seats that turned similarly to a merry-go-round.

'I'll go on it with you, Mary.' Daisy made this offer. 'Annapolly would probably like that one as well.'

Annapolly was indeed keen. In the end all three girls lined up for the ride with their father. Jess smiled at the picture of Dan's strong imposing back as he waited for the ride with his three daughters.

'Let's watch Luke and Rob have their fun while we wait, Ella.' Jess pushed the stroller to a vantage point and watched Luke and Rob get into one of the cross-barred seats. Moments later the ride had begun and they were climbing high into the sky as the speed of the ride picked up.

Two rotations later there was a sickening, grinding sound. The ride operator shouted, and the ride came to a jarring stop with occupants of a lot of the cages shrieking in shock.

'Oh my God.' Luke and Rob were stuck right at the top of the ride. Dan's boys were *not safe* up there. They weren't in a full locking cage. There was nothing but a cross bar keeping them secure while they dangled there.

Ella had fallen asleep in the stroller. Dan was stuck on the other ride with his daughters.

Jess caught the eye of a local woman

nearby. 'Mrs O'Donnell, would you please watch my daughter? My charges are stuck up there.'

The kindly middle-aged woman took charge of Ella's stroller, and Jess rushed to the base of the ride. She yelled up: 'I'm here, Luke and Rob. Don't move!'

'I don't like this, Jess.' Rob's voice quavered. 'It's all shaking.'

Jess didn't like it either, and she caught sight of the ride manager who seemed to be doing nothing but wringing his hands while another man ineffectively prodded at the gear mechanism of the ride. Jess searched both boys' faces before she yelled out again.

'Luke's there with you, Rob. He's not going to let anything happen to either of you, are you, Luke?'

She held her breath as she waited for Luke's answer, and her heart softened with gratitude as he told his brother fiercely that he'd hold on to him all day up there if need be.

'We're not going to fall, Rob. All we have to do is be sensible, and hang on tight if things start banging about again.'

Luke's words were stern. In that moment Jess saw more of Dan in the boy than she ever had. And she saw what he was holding back, too, holding back his own concerns, and the knowledge that despite his assurances to Rob they *weren't* safe.

Jess strode to the ride manager. 'What's happened here? Those are my charges at the top of the ride.'

'It's nothing. Please step aside.' The manager cast a trapped look her way. 'We'll have this fixed in a moment.'

The other man shook his head. 'I really think we need to call in a crane to get them all off the ride. I don't like how this break looks here.' He pointed to what Jess had already seen, a sheared-off piece of metal, a bunch of cogs out of alignment.

A potential serious accident waiting to happen?

'Call for a crane, now.' Jess's words were harsh, low.

There were other people beginning to gather around as they realised the ride wasn't merely temporarily paused for some reason.

The manager glared at Jess before the other man said in a low tone, 'It'll be bad if any of them panic or try to climb down, Jack. Call for the crane.'

Jess stood close by until she'd heard the call go through. Once it had she spoke to Luke and Rob again, told them their dad would be here very soon. Dan's ride had been stopped as well and he was coming over. 'A crane's on the way to get you all down.'

Once she'd told the boys this, Jess pulled out her own mobile phone and called the police. She briefly explained what had happened and asked them to attend.

Things moved quickly after that. The crane and the police arrived. Dan and the girls joined Jess, and she quickly explained the situation and took charge of the girls while Dan called out to his sons. Jess retrieved her sleeping daughter from Mrs O'Donnell, thanked her, and rejoined Dan.

'Oh, I don't want to watch this.' But Jess did watch, and prayed and held on to Dan's arm until Rob and Luke were safely transferred from the top of the ride to the crane, and from there to ground level.

'You're all right?' Dan pulled them both aside and listened as Rob spilled out how scary it had been.

'Luke was great with him, Dan.' Jess spoke quietly. 'He kept Rob calm, reassured him up there until you could get here from the other ride.'

'Thanks, Luke.' Dan hugged both sons before he released them. 'I need to speak with the ride manager, and then the police. This shouldn't have happened and I want to know why it did.'

It was Luke who held on to his father's arm. 'Dad — Jess was the one who made them get a crane in, and called the police on them.'

'Thanks.' Dan met Jess's gaze briefly before he strode to where the police were questioning the ride manager and his assistant.

'Dad's gonna kick heads.' Rob said it with a hint of ghoulish glee.

'I'm so relieved you're all right, Rob.' Jess spoke from the depths of her heart, but she also caught Luke's gaze and smiled before she could stop herself, and Luke . . . almost smiled before he looked away.

Dan did what he had to do and then came back to join them. 'I've had quite enough of this place. The police have my number. Let's go home.'

CHAPTER NINE

'Dad's really stressed about what happened with that ride.' Daisy made this observation to Jess later. 'He's been on the phone in his den with the police and stuff like that half the afternoon. If he's not taking phone calls, he's checking on Luke and Rob. They're all right though, aren't they, Jess?'

'Yes, Daisy. They're okay.' Jess thought in truth that the boys were probably more resilient about the whole thing than the adults had been. They'd had a fright. In the end nothing terrible had come of it and they'd got over it. Rob had already been on the phone bragging to the new friends he and Luke had met at the fair about the excitement of being stuck up there.

But Dan had to deal with getting to the bottom of what had gone wrong, and why, and work with the police and others to ensure responsibility was taken for the incident, and that there wouldn't be a repeat. Meanwhile, Jess needed to feed everyone and get the children into bed, at least the younger ones, because that was *her* job. 'I must put something on for dinner. I confess I've been a bit distracted, too. It was a little frightening while they were stuck up there.'

'You should give us all pizza.' Daisy glanced outside to where Luke and Rob were sitting on the veranda.

The boys were talking, rather than riding their bikes. Maybe they'd had enough excitement for one day, too.

Daisy went on. 'Dad usually treats everyone if we've had a rough day. He won't want to eat until later, though.' She added with calm unconcern for exposing her father's finer feelings, 'His guts get in a total knot over stuff like this.'

They did end up treating the children with pizza. Jess said she might 'like to eat a bit later if that would suit Dan' and he readily agreed and disappeared back into his den to try to catch up on his Sydney-related workload while Jess got everyone sorted for bed.

Luke, for once, left his door open while Jess took care of the smaller children. When they were all in their rooms, she hesitated for a moment and then briefly poked her head in. 'You're all right, Luke? No after effects from that drama earlier today?'

'Yeah, I'm okay.' He seemed a bit at a loss.

A sound came through the baby monitor in Jess's pocket. 'I'd better go check on that. I guess Ella's going to take more than one tucking in tonight to get her to sleep.'

Jess checked on her daughter, settled her and then took care of some laundry and cleared up the bathrooms and kitchen before she finally went in search of Dan. She met him as he was returning from checking on the children.

'They're all asleep.' He shoved a hand through his hair.

It was already ruffled from, Jess assumed, several such treatments. She tried not to think about being the one to do the ruffling. 'You look fed up, and justifiably so. What have the police had to say about the problem with the ride?'

'There will definitely be a hefty fine for the owners and a probable suspension of licence. The problem appears to have resulted from negligence rather than any tolerable wear and tear or other issues.'

'Then I hope they receive the harshest fine and punishment possible.' Jess drew a breath. 'Shall I order us some pizza now, Dan?'

'Actually I got on the phone before I checked on the kids. It should be here soon. Can we eat it on a desert island where there's nothing at all to bug us or cause concern? You know, I really could do with just a couple of hours where I could totally relax.' As the words left his mouth, Dan frowned. 'And so could you. I'm sorry. With what happened to Luke and Rob on that ride I forgot you were waiting on a call from my solicitor today.'

'It's okay.' That news hadn't come, and it could wait another day. 'I think we've had enough to contend with for today.'

Jess was trying so hard, but she *was* still aware of Dan as a man. Remembrance of the kiss they'd shared hovered constantly on the edge of her thoughts, lifting that awareness to a higher level, making her long for more even though she knew how foolish it was to do that.

Why had she let Dan kiss her when she knew it could only end in hurt for her because he didn't have anything in his heart?

'I don't know of any nearby desert islands.' Jess tried for a light smile. 'When Daisy wants to escape she goes into the tree house.'

Just as the doorbell rang Dan gave Jess a considering look.

159

He strode to the door and opened up, and came back a moment later with the pizza. 'Why not? There's a bottle of sparkling grape juice in the fridge. We'll eat pizza and drink that and get away from the day for a bit.'

When Jess simply looked at him, he added, 'You have the baby monitor, and you know once my lot fall asleep nothing short of a fire-alarm situation would wake them so we won't be worrying about them.'

And it would get them both out of the house, and potentially give Dan's 'guts' a chance to settle down. 'I've never eaten a meal in a tree house.'

When they climbed up there, Jess drew a breath. 'Here we are, then.'

'Yes. Looks like Daisy's had a tea party or something up here.' Dan's glance roved the room and he fell silent.

Jess's gaze followed Dan's to a picnic blanket spread across the floor. Scatter cushions to lean on. Flowers from the garden picked with girlish hands and stuffed into a plastic tumbler. They were already wilted.

'How —' She couldn't very well say romantic though that was the word that sprang to mind. 'How lovely the view is through the cut-away window. You can see heaps of stars.'

Jess pretended an extreme rate of interest in those stars while Dan set down the boxes of pizza in complete silence. After a moment she heard the fizz as he opened the bottle of sparkling grape juice and the sound as he poured it into the plastic tumblers they'd brought out and she knew she had to turn around.

Dan's ears were red again. And Jess felt as though she were on a date, which was quite ridiculous. Yet they were here, secluded, nothing but each other's company and a house full of children not at all far away, but they might as well have been miles away.

'We don't have to do this, Dan —'

'At least it's quiet out here —' He broke off and handed her one of the cups.

It wasn't real wine, but all Jess could think about was being kissed anyway.

Reclining back on those scatter cushions and being kissed by Dan. 'It's — it's good that it's quiet. For the peace of it, I mean.' That was what she *should* mean.

She took the sparkling juice and sat, and she would just have to stop thinking about this being a romantic setting. It was a children's tree cubby house. How *could* that even be romantic?

Jess reached for the first pizza box. 'Well,

I'm certainly hungry. How about you?'

'It does smell good.' Dan reached for a slice of pizza.

Their hands brushed.

Not a big deal, Jess.

They ate in silence for a minute or two.

'How are things progressing with your Sydney client?' Jess hadn't asked for a few days, but prior to the fiasco at the fair today Dan had been working from home more.

In the back of her mind where all the tensions and concerns about the future lurked, a part of Jess hadn't wanted to ask in case Dan had almost resolved things and wouldn't need her for much longer. She wasn't ready to face yet another worry over finances. She wasn't ready to leave . . . Dan.

Dan finished his slice of pizza and selected another before offering the box to her. 'I think my clients are close to being fully assessed now. A purchase offer shouldn't be too far away.'

'You won't need my help for much longer, then.' Jess forced herself to smile. She would be fine. She and Ella had made it this far and they would go on making it whether Jess lost this work, whether she also lost their cottage or not. Of course they would be fine.

'For at least another month, Jess, if you

can do it.' Dan drew a breath. 'I'll cope without you if you can't commit for that long. I don't want to get in the way of other plans you might need to make, but if you *can* stick at it for another month it'll give me time to wrap up this problem, get the kids started at school, and hopefully for things to start to settle down. I've really appreciated all your help, including the things you've done in terms of housekeeping.'

'I hope I can find enough work in Randurra to stay here, Dan. That's what I'll be aiming for. Actually I'd like to ask for half of tomorrow off to do some more door knocking if that's all right?'

He agreed straight away, and Jess went on.

'I'll stay on with you another month if at all possible.' It was Jess's turn to draw a breath before she went on. 'I don't feel comfortable asking you for help finding out my rights regarding the cottage.'

'You're independent. I understand that.' His glance drifted over the chunky wooden necklace that matched the bangles on her arm, and down to the cleft between her breasts before he looked away. 'But it was easy for me to get that help for you, and I wanted to.'

'Thank you, Dan. I do appreciate it.' Jess's

skin warmed as though Dan had touched her, and she became aware very suddenly that the only sounds around them were of night insects and the occasional hoot of an owl somewhere in the distance. They were very alone out here, whether there were children sleeping in the house or not. They were alone and Jess didn't think she was the only one aware of it . . .

'That was a nice break.' Jess gathered the used plates together and piled them on top of the pizza boxes and hoped she didn't sound as desperate to escape her thoughts as she was. 'I'll take these in and get Ella and head home.'

'Leave it.' Dan stilled her movements by the simple expedient of laying his hand over hers. 'It can stay here until morning but you're right. It's time to go in.'

They couldn't stay out here and drift as they had done. If they did, the drifting *would* end in kisses. The truth of that was in Dan's eyes, and she didn't want him to reject her twice.

So they went inside and Jess got Ella and put her in the car, drove home and sent Dan a text message that they'd arrived safe and sound. She put Ella to bed and climbed into her own bed and while she waited for sleep to come she did what she could to toughen her resolve.

She *had* let herself care too much about Dan, and she'd pushed back her concerns about losing her home and tried not to think about them because she didn't want to face the choices she might have to make to survive. Moving out of Randurra. Getting work outside the childcare industry that would separate her from Ella.

Jess had to knock on more doors, and see what work she could find. She had to get ready for whatever Dan's solicitor might tell her, have her plans already in train to deal with whatever life threw down.

And she had to push aside any feelings she might think she had towards Dan that were not about work.

Jess could do it all alone. She *had been* standing alone. And she would go on standing alone. For herself, and for Ella. That was all. Her determination had nothing to do with pushing people away to keep herself safe.

Jess was the one who'd been pushed away by Peter Rosche, and in the end Dan was doing that to her, too. He wanted her as a daycare mum, but he did not want her for herself.

Well, Jess did not need him in that way.
She didn't!

CHAPTER TEN

The next day dawned clear and sunny with a gentle breeze taking the edge off the heat. In the afternoon Dan suggested a walk to the dam on the property to try to catch yabbies for a bit of fun.

'Daddy, Daddy, I've got one. What do I do?' Mary yelled the words as her line of string went tight in the muddy water.

The children were spread out around one side of the dam with bits of sausage tied to pieces of string, and the string tied to sticks planted in the mud at the edge of the water. Rob and Luke had managed to resist throwing dried mud clods into the water. They'd thrown them up the bank instead.

As mini excursions went, Jess thought this one was rather inventive, and Dan had seemed happy to forfeit the time in his office to spend it with the children, instead.

Dan went to Mary's side and put his hand over hers. He had an old plastic colander from the kitchen to use as a net. 'We just pull the string in gently like this until we can see the yabby in the shallow water. He's a lot like a crab except long and thinner. He'll hold on to the meat with his pincers. Once we have him close, we'll scoop him up.'

They pulled. They saw the yabby. They scooped and all had a good look at him.

'Sausage works pretty well to catch them with, Dad.' Daisy sounded surprised. 'But you said that smelly older meat would work even better?'

'Yes. I'm fairly sure.'

Jess leaned close to Dan's ear to whisper, 'You're an expert now that you've been on the Internet to find out all about it.'

'Totally.' Dan turned his head and his lips came close to brushing her cheek.

Dan's eyes darkened and his gaze dropped to her lips before he quickly turned his attention to releasing the yabby so they could all watch it back itself into the water and disappear. He missed the furious look that Luke cast their way, but Jess didn't, and she wished she could explain to Luke —

What? That there was nothing between her and Dan? When all Dan needed to do was come anywhere near her and she all but melted, and she couldn't seem to do a thing about it no matter how hard she tried!

Jess moved away from Dan and she took care to keep her distance for the next hour that they stayed, catching and releasing yabbies. Rob wanted to keep them and cook some but Dan said no.

'I'm not sure if they'd be safe to eat,' he said, 'and I don't think I'd be all that keen to cook them anyway. But we'll have a campfire tonight, Rob. I checked the weather report and we can do it in a safe spot in the backyard.'

Ella had fallen asleep in the stroller under the shade of a gumtree.

Jess helped gather everything up and they all made their way back to the house. Rob and Luke got in a bit of a spat with each other over something Jess didn't hear, shoving and pushing. Dan broke them up and looked frustrated but seemed to push all his feelings inside. Where did the tension go when he did that?

Mary asked a question and Ella started to wake up in the stroller, and then they were back at the house and Jess didn't get time to try to figure anything else out.

They cleaned up, and got ready for their outdoor supervised campfire in the backyard. Dan had asked Jess to help him, and it was her job to do whatever he needed whether there were tensions in the air, or not.

'Grubs are fun.' Rob twisted another piece of dough around his stick, closed it over the end and held it out to the fire's flames. 'I'm going to pour even more golden syrup into this one when it's cooked.'

'You're already covered in the stuff.' Luke made this observation while he prepared another grub stick for himself.

'Why are they called grubs?' Daisy wanted to know.

'Because they look like witchetty grubs that can be eaten as bush tucker.' Jess hadn't needed to look on the Internet to know that one. The grubs had been her idea.

'I never thought Dad would let us eat things cooked on sticks.' Rob turned his stick over the flames again. 'Even if it is just dough, it tastes really good.'

'Yeah, well, he hasn't got any scruples when it comes to some people and what they want to do.' Luke muttered the words beneath his breath, but Jess heard them, and a glance at Dan's face showed that he had, too.

'Go to your room, Luke. That was completely uncalled for. You're done here for the night.' Dan spoke the words quietly.

169

Luke stared at his father for a moment before he threw his stick into the fire and stormed inside.

Rob threw a glance at his father. 'I didn't mean to get him in trouble.'

'Leave it, Rob. It's nothing to do with you.'

The family event went on, but all the pleasure had gone out of it for Jess. The campfire dwindled. One by one the children made their way inside to wash and get into bed and then it was just Jess and Dan as he dumped sand over the coals.

'I'll get my sleeping girl and head home, Dan.' She tried to find something neutral to say. 'It's good that you were able to spare the time from your work for this afternoon and evening. You'll have another busy day in your office or in Sydney tomorrow.'

Something in his face made Jess pause.

'The audit is finished. I can spend the remainder of the school holidays at home and do what I can to get the kids in a good place about starting their classes.'

'Well, that's great.' Dan had asked for a month more from Jess, but with the pressure removed things would be different for him. 'You'll be okay now, Dan. You'll get on with things and the children will really settle in here.'

'That sounded rather like a goodbye.' His

gaze searched her face.

'You won't need my help any more.' That was the thing. 'I can't let you keep paying me to work here when that's the case.'

'I want to keep you working for me, Jess.'

'I'll be okay. The regular children will be back with me as of Saturday and I have new ones starting then as well.'

'That's good, Jess. But I do still want you here.' Dan drew a breath. 'Sometimes trying to balance everything is, well, it's hard. The ongoing work I mentioned before, help with housekeeping and even watching Annapolly a couple of days once the others are back in school is something I think I'd really like.'

'I'll help you, Dan.' If he still needed her. 'Of course I will for as long as you want me.'

Jess couldn't say otherwise anyway. She didn't have the luxury of that choice.

Dan blew out a deep breath. 'Good. That's really good.' He didn't want to let Jess know just how relieved he felt. Dan wasn't sure he wanted to think about the level of relief himself. For tonight all he was prepared to consider was that he still needed her help.

He was thinking of his children, making sure things were in a good place for them. Helping Jess in the process, and helping

171

himself because what he'd admitted to her was true.

And Luke, Dan? Are you thinking of Luke when you make this decision?

Luke would just have to respect Dan's choice. Dan hadn't been in to see his son after sending him inside. He would check on him before he turned in, but if Luke was still awake he didn't expect to make any progress trying to talk to him.

You're avoiding even trying to do that because you don't want to have to confront what Luke is feeling. He's jealous that you want to express interest in someone other than his mother. He doesn't want you replacing Rebecca with . . . Jess.

Dan didn't want to pursue that path at all. That was what Luke didn't seem to understand. Dan had fought his attraction to Jess and he was still fighting it.

'Goodnight, Jess.' He tried not to sound distant but simply professional. He wasn't sure whether or not he succeeded.

'Goodnight, Dan. I guess I'll see you in the morning.' She got to her feet and quickly left him.

CHAPTER ELEVEN

'I'm sorry.' Jess drew a shaken breath. 'I'm just really shocked. I can't believe this.'

But the proof stood in front of her. A man and a woman in their mid-fifties who'd climbed from their car outside Jess's cottage just as she waved off the last of her charges and started to turn to go back inside.

It was Saturday. Jess had Ella in her arms, and as the woman looked from Jess to her baby daughter moisture pooled in her eyes and a hopeful smile came over her face.

'We're sorry to spring ourselves on you this way.' The man also seemed shaken, but he offered Jess a very sincere glance before he went on. 'There's a bit to talk about, if you'd be willing. Once we learned you were supposed to be here, we decided to drive out from Sydney. We weren't even sure if we'd be able to find you or if it was all real.'

They'd introduced themselves as Dalia

and George Rosche. They were Peter's parents, if what they were saying was true, and they'd hired a private investigator to track him down. They hadn't succeeded, but the investigator had found out about the cottage Peter purchased for Jess, and had learned that a young woman lived there with her baby daughter.

'What made you think — ?' Jess hesitated, uncertain how to put it.

'That we might find a grandchild here?' Dalia blinked. 'Peter got drunk at our house a year ago. He'd brought another man with him, some friend. We heard him tell the man that, well, that he was a father but he'd made sure he'd never have to be responsible for it. Ever since then we've been asking ourselves how we could find you.'

The words about her son had been harsh, but behind them Jess could sense shame, and . . . hope to know her granddaughter?

Jess laid her hand on the older woman's arm. 'You're not responsible for Peter's actions, Mrs Rosche. I think perhaps we should go inside.'

She made tea for the couple. George Rosche looked a lot like Peter, but the similarities appeared to finish on the surface.

George started the conversation. 'We realise you don't owe us anything, Jessica. Is it okay to call you that?'

'Of course.' Jess set Ella down and let her crawl around the floor.

'And you must call us Dalia and George,' Peter's father went on. 'We're hoping that, despite Peter's behaviour towards you, you might allow us to play a part as grandparents in your daughter's life.'

'I — I don't know what to say.' Jess didn't know how to deal with the knot of surprise and hope that had tightened into a fist in the middle of her chest. She drew a breath and whispered, 'Do you really want to?'

They talked for three hours. It was an emotional three hours for Jess, for the grandparents, but not for Ella, who played happily about the cottage and didn't realise she was the centre of some very focused and hopeful attention from this older couple.

Jess changed her daughter while George and Dalia took a moment to speak quietly in the kitchen. When she came back she drew another deep breath and handed Ella into Dalia's arms. The older woman held the little girl while silent tears ran down her face.

George had his moment, too, his large hands holding Ella awkwardly before he noisily cleared his throat and handed her back to Jess.

'I think you really mean what you've been saying.' Jess sought Dalia's eyes. 'I hope you'll forgive my doubts, but Peter —'

'Was not at all kind to you.' It was George who completed the sentence. 'Our son bought this cottage for you, but he made an agreement about back rates on it with the local council.'

'I signed an agreement to stay out of Peter's life in return for him buying me this cottage.' Jess could see no harm in admitting it.

'And he double-crossed you by hiding those back rates.' Dalia closed her eyes briefly before she turned to her husband. 'We have to make this right, George. We can't allow this young woman to be treated like that by our son.'

They offered to pay off the back rates debt.

'I can't let you do that. It's not your responsibility.'

'We can talk about that later.' George cleared his throat. 'We've probably taken up enough of your time for today but we appreciate meeting you and our granddaughter.'

'It has been a bit of a surprise.' But Jess didn't want to lose these people. They were grandparents who wanted to know Ella. Jess had to give that a chance.

'Are you staying overnight in the area?' she ventured.

'We have a room booked at the motel in the centre of town.' Dalia got to her feet. 'Come, George. We've worn the poor girl to a frazzle and our granddaughter is getting sleepy.' She turned to Jess. 'Would you allow us to come again tomorrow? You'll need time to think about all of this but we truly would like to get to know you, and have a chance to contribute at least a little to our granddaughter's life if you'll let us.'

Jess agreed to a second visit and explained that it would have to be quite early, as she had to work elsewhere the next day. And she did need time to think as well. They exchanged mobile phone numbers, and the older couple went on their way. Jess tucked Ella into her cot, and, once her daughter was asleep, turned in herself.

She couldn't let these people pay off her debt. That would just be wrong. But to have them as part of Ella's life, loving grandparents who wanted to know their granddaughter? That would be so wonderful for Ella.

A little prickle of loneliness stabbed at Jess's heart. Because this would be great for her daughter, but *Jess* wasn't any relation to George and Dalia. And of course that didn't matter. She had a chance to have something special for Ella. That was what counted.

So go to sleep, Jess Baker. Tomorrow you have grandparents visiting your daughter again.

'It's Aunt Adele and Uncle Clive!' Rob shouted and a troop of Frazier children raced off the veranda to meet the car.

Jess was just arriving, too.

Dan hadn't exactly been waiting on the veranda for Jess's arrival. He'd been supervising the children, he told himself.

'Hey, Dan. We thought we'd surprise you.' Adele called the words as she climbed out of the car.

The children swarmed around her and Clive, all talking at once, even Luke.

'I thought you were both still travelling.' With one part of him, Dan watched Jess getting Ella out of the car as he smiled at the visitors. 'It's great to see you, though.'

Adele explained that they'd finished their trip a little early. Her hand covered her tummy for a moment before Clive took over the conversation.

'We had the time so we decided to drive

down, Dan.' Clive's glance shifted to Jess and her daughter.

'Come meet my sister and brother-in-law, Jess.' Dan walked to Jess's side. 'Adele, Clive, this is Jess Baker. Jess has been providing childcare and housekeeping for me while I handled a work crisis that blew up in Sydney.'

'Oh.' Adele took Jess's hand and shook firmly while Clive nodded and smiled. Adele glanced back to Dan. 'How did that happen? You were supposed to be able to take things easy while you got settled in.'

Dan explained and they all went inside. Adele had brought small treats for the children, and handed those out before she and her husband settled with Dan and Jess in the kitchen for cups of tea.

Jess made the drinks and would have left them to it. 'I can watch the children while you all catch up.'

'Stay.' Adele smiled. 'It would be nice to get to know you.'

At first Dan thought Jess might seem a bit overwhelmed because of the sudden arrival of his relatives, but there seemed to be something deeper disturbing her, as though she'd already had some kind of shock.

Well, she's worried about losing her cottage. That's enough to make anyone shocked.

Dan had been thinking about that. He wanted to help. There had to be some way that they could work something out.

Just what are you asking yourself, Dan?

'Dan? I asked whether you'd allow it?' Adele's prompting made Dan replay the part of the conversation that hadn't fully registered because he'd allowed his thoughts to wander.

'You want to take the children overnight to Sydney?' He blinked.

'It would be nice to spoil them a little, and it would give you a break.' Adele's face softened as she half turned her head to glance behind her into the living room. 'I don't want to lose being part of their lives now that you've moved and don't need my occasional help with childcare.'

She glanced again at Jess before she turned back to her brother. 'And I'm glad you've finally got help with some of the care and housekeeping. It's way too much for someone who's working full time as well.'

'Can we go, Dad? Please, please, please?' Mary had heard the invitation and come into the kitchen. In moments, four other Fraziers had added their hopes to the mix.

Dan agreed. A flurry of packing followed and it seemed before he could blink Adele had piled them all into Dan's van. She left her car behind to be collected when they brought the children back.

Dan and Jess stood on the veranda in a sudden silence broken only by the sound of Ella crawling to Jess and making a little bewildered sound as if to ask, 'What was all that about?'

'It's all right, Ella. They've just gone for a visit with their aunt and uncle.' Jess picked up the little girl and stroked her hand over Ella's soft wispy hair. 'You keep getting shocked by strange people turning up, don't you?'

While Dan drew a breath to ask what she meant, Jess turned her head and spoke to him.

'With your family gone for two days, did you still want me, Dan?'

More with each passing day.

'Yes.' He cleared his throat and cast about for an excuse — *for the things he'd been holding off doing because it was too hard with heaps of children.* 'Any chance you'd like to help me with some light yard work this morning? And maybe get ahead with some baking this afternoon while I flatten all the moving boxes and arrange to have them taken away for recycling? I hadn't realised Adele might miss the children like that.'

Jess smiled and bounced Ella in her arms.

'I liked her, Dan. She seemed a really good sort. Your brother-in-law, too.'

She rolled her sleeves up, then. Metaphorically at least. She slathered Ella in sun block, put a big hat on her and placed her in the playpen in the shade, and they set to work while the sun was still low in the sky.

CHAPTER TWELVE

'Ella's down for the count. She napped earlier, but apparently watching people carrying boxes is exhausting work for a one-year-old.' Jess made the observation as she stepped into the living room. 'I'll try to get a bit more work done, Dan, before I go home —'

'Leave it for tonight.' Dan glanced up from where he'd been pressing buttons on the TV remote to change channels. 'In fact, would you like to watch some television with me?'

Jess hesitated and then, when she glanced at the screen, said, 'Is that show what I think it is?'

He'd found an old comedy show that Jess loved. Dan gestured to the seat beside him on the couch. 'Come and watch it. We've worked hard enough today to earn it.'

They had, Jess justified, and plopped down beside him. She refused to think about the wisdom or otherwise of what she was doing.

One comedy show led to another, and then to a discussion about ones they liked best, and Dan dug through the family's DVD collection. They selected two movies. For the second one, Jess brought cocoa and cookies and somehow they ended up sitting closer. She could feel Dan's shoulder and arm against her side.

There were a dozen reasons why she should go home. Her response to Dan's nearness was top of the list but she couldn't make herself get up, or say the words. And the longer she stayed there, the more aware of Dan she became, and the more she sensed that he was equally aware of her.

Yet Dan had pushed her away, and he hadn't wanted the complication. Oh, Jess didn't know what to make of her feelings, or of what she thought she might sense in him.

At about the halfway point of the story, Dan glanced her way and she turned her head. He clicked off the television and tossed the remote down. 'What are we going to do, Jess? I thought I was making it up, that it couldn't be all that it is, that I couldn't . . . want you as much as I do, but it just doesn't go away, does it?'

'No.' His words to her had been so sincere. Jess might have held her own need at bay if it hadn't been for that. She might have held away from him. 'It doesn't go away.'

He kissed her then, and Jess wound her arms around his neck and kissed him back. She wanted him. She had done for ages, since they first met really, and she was tired of fighting her feelings, tired of holding back when all she wanted and needed was to be in his arms. In some ways she needed that even more because of Luke's resistance to her presence in his father's life.

Dan raised his lips from hers. 'You work for me, Jess, and you're so much younger. I don't want to make you feel —'

Don't do it, Jessica. Don't invest yourself emotionally, and don't let this end up where it wants to end physically. It won't mean the same thing to him.

'I want this, Dan.' Jess spoke firmly. 'I want to be in your arms tonight while it's just us. It doesn't have to be more than that. Just . . . tonight.'

Jess pushed aside her concerns and told herself to see it as a gift.

Dan stroked her hair away from her face with his hand and his gaze sought hers. There *were* emotions in his eyes. Questions, concerns, need and an edge of uncertainty.

185

He too seemed to push it all aside. He drew a deep breath and their kisses deepened.

Jess melted into his arms in a tangle of emotions that she wouldn't face. Not now. Not yet. Her hands touched his chest through the cloth of his shirt. His muscles were firm beneath her fingertips. He smelled of blunted aftershave and sunshine and Dan. She closed her eyes and didn't even notice that the sweetness of his kisses had pushed through the walls she'd shored up around her heart.

'Jess.' Dan rose from the couch where he'd been kissing her. He needed to take her to his bed and take what they'd begun to its fulfilment and after that . . .

After that it would be over. Jess had said it. 'Just tonight.' She knew what she wanted, and for tonight, while his children weren't here, what harm were they doing?

Dan pushed his own thoughts down. He only wanted to focus on the moment. If he was avoiding issues, that was one more thing he didn't want to acknowledge.

He threw back the cover on his bed and Jess stood at the edge of it. He took her hands and lifted them to his chest. She pushed his shirt over his head and her nails scraped lightly over his skin. Need rushed through Dan in a tight wave.

His hands shook as he removed Jess's sleeveless top. A knot tightened inside him but Jess looked into his eyes, and her gaze was soft and welcoming.

Jess pushed her skirt down over her hips, and Dan removed the rest of their clothes slowly, touching every part of her as it was revealed. He drew her down on the bed and took her into his arms . . .

'Dan. Please.' Jess's hands clasped his shoulders and she acknowledged her need for his hold and his touch and his possession.

His eyes were soft and filled with desire, blurred with passion held in check. Jess wanted him to give all of that to her, and, if she was fooling herself that she would still hold that gift tomorrow, she couldn't care. She needed this. The chance to give herself to him and have him give himself to her. She needed it more than she wanted to acknowledge.

So she didn't. She just opened her arms to him, and when he led them to their zenith Jess looked into his eyes and those walls built around her heart didn't hold together as well as they should. She had a suspicion that she might have let Dan find his way further into all those parts of herself that she'd needed to protect after Peter than she'd meant to.

'Stay, Jess.' His hands soothed her, stroked across her body even as he pushed out a breath and a well of tension that had perhaps been in both of them, washed away on their tide of fulfilment. Lethargy followed for Jess.

She tucked her head against his chest and his arms came around her. Dan eased into sleep and she lay there and closed her eyes. She didn't want to think because there had been too much thinking about too many things in her life and she had not found any answers. Now she had hope with Ella's grandparents and she would survive at whatever home she found to live in.

Would she go on working for Dan? Was it best to do that, or to walk away after what had happened tonight?

How *could* she walk away when he was helping her to afford to live by the income his employment provided?

She should have thought of that before she made love with him! But Jess couldn't regret it. She pressed her face to his chest and she didn't regret any of it.

'Good morning. I woke up because of Ella so I thought I'd get started early on breakfast and then I've written a shopping list. If you'll give me the card, I'll take Ella with me to the supermarket. You'll need to be well supplied for when the children get back, and your sister and brother-in-law might decide to stay as well.'

Jess put a cup of tea in front of Dan and pushed the breakfast cereal and milk his way. She bent to pick Ella up off the floor, sat down with her and started to spoon baby cereal into her mouth.

Jess's head was bent over the task and she was going determinedly about her business, but her hand shook as she fed her daughter.

'Jess.' Dan didn't know what to say to her. He was shocked by how he had felt when they made love. Dan had told himself it was just about sex. He was attracted to her. It had been a long time. He'd . . . justified it in that way. But it hadn't felt like just sex. He didn't know what he had felt.

'Du — du-u-u!' Ella wriggled on Jess's lap and Jess set her down on the floor.

She still didn't meet Dan's gaze. What could he say to her? How did he reassure her that what happened — ? Dan didn't even know what he wanted to say. What they'd shared had stunned him, but it had been . . . ill advised. And Dan felt guilt, and didn't want to have to confront that feeling.

'Du — Da-a-a —'

Dan glanced down in just enough time to see Ella pull herself up on the leg of the chair Jess was sitting on. She reached out first one hand towards him and then the other.

Ella tottered forward.

Jess gasped and held her breath.

Dan shot his hands out. 'Come on, Ella. Look what you're doing. You're walking. All by yourself.'

Ella got three and a half steps in before she seemed to realise that she was on her feet, and started to wonder how she was doing it. Dan caught her up just as her legs wobbled, and praised her for her amazing efforts.

'Did you see that, Jess? She walked.' Even in the face of this morning's concerns, Dan couldn't help but grin.

'I've been waiting for this moment.' Jess's words were filled with pride, and then her voice turned husky as Dan passed Ella to her and she cuddled her daughter close. 'What a good girl you are, Ella.'

Ella gave a baby laugh and cuddled back, but Jess still had the strangest look on her face. It had come the moment she saw Ella walking to Dan.

Dan looked at her with her daughter in her arms, and he thought about Ella walking to him and all the memories of all of his children, and he wondered what it would be like to have a child . . . with Jess?

The thought so startled him that he fell silent. Did he *want* to have a child with Jess? That would mean that he wanted —

Dan's mobile phone rang. The caller was Adele. 'Hello, Adele. How are you? How are the children? Is everything okay?'

He sounded quite normal, Dan thought. Not like a man asking himself questions that he'd believed were answered four years ago.

'Yes, we're all fine. Just letting you know we'll be back today at about five.' Adele cleared her throat. 'And that we, sort of, well, shopped a little.'

'No problem.' Dan could feel his ears turning red, as though some part of him felt that his sister would know that Jess was here holding her daughter, and that Dan had made love to Jess last night.

Well, now it was today and they had their lives to get on with. They weren't going to cross those boundaries again. They'd both agreed about that so Dan didn't have to psychoanalyse *or* regret.

'I'll see you later, Dan.' Adele's tone was a little questioning, but she ended the call without saying more.

He set the phone down. Of course Adele

would wonder. He hadn't asked to speak to any of the children or what they'd been buying or any of the things he'd normally have done.

'I — I should get busy with some housekeeping, Dan. It's too early to go to the shops.' Jess heard the tentative edge to her tone as she addressed him, and forced her chin up. She couldn't fall apart. Not now. Not because of last night. Not because Ella had walked to Dan and Jess's heart, those walls around her heart, had taken one final big shake and crashed down.

Ella had reached out to him with total trust and taken her first steps to him.

Jess had reached out to him last night and taken a step with him too. She'd thought she had it under control, but she hadn't. Because when she watched Ella walk to Dan, it hit Jess just why *she* had felt so deeply about what they had shared last night. Why she had needed it and longed for it so much.

She'd fallen in love with him! All the way in, heart, soul, the whole lot. She hadn't realised she was doing it and now she had and she had to *undo* it! She couldn't love Dan. Not like that. He wouldn't give back in the same way and she'd end up so hurt.

Been there, done that, and Peter Rosche

192

had turned out not to even be the man Jess had thought she'd fallen for.

Dan was Dan. Jess had no doubt that he was exactly who he was. Her complete lack of doubt was what should concern her most of all. Dan was a man who'd loved and lost and would never love again. Eighteen years with his Rebecca. How *could* he ever move past that amount of history with a woman he had loved utterly?

'I apologise, Jess.' Dan's low words weren't really unexpected.

They still hurt, and wasn't that silly? But Jess didn't want to hear him apologise. She wanted him to refuse to say sorry for any aspect of last night, to want to keep her and find some means to take their relationship forward . . .

'There's no need to say anything.' There was no need for Jess to think such thoughts, either. It wasn't going to happen. Not in a million billion years.

'I think there is.' His mouth tightened. 'You work for me. I shouldn't have put you in a position that could make you uncom-fortable with me afterwards, could risk that. I don't want to lose you as the carer for the children. Even when they're back in school I want at least two days a week —'

'What happened was a joint decision.' Jess

had walked into it, eyes open. She'd made up her mind what she wanted. But her *heart* hadn't realised what it was letting itself in for.

Dan was worried that she'd feel too uncomfortable to stay with him — and he wanted her to stay on more permanently! A frown came to her brows as Jess started to think what that would be like, now. She loved Dan. She was *in love with* Dan.

And he *liked* her. He wanted her to help him with housework and the children. He didn't want her for herself.

It was still work, and Jess cared about his children, even the difficult Luke.

Jess drew herself up. 'This job matters to me. I like knowing that I'm helping you. If you're happy to carry on, I don't see why we can't.'

He blew out a breath and his face for a moment reflected relief.

Because he was trying to back away from what happened last night, Jessica, and without losing you for his children. Don't read anything more than that into it.

Dan might even have been concerned how she would react to a perceived breach of their employer/employee relationship, but it had been a joint choice.

Jess excused herself then. There was nothing more to be said. She'd fallen in love in a totally unsuitable way with a man who didn't love her back and never would.

With Ella scooped into her arms, Jess took her daughter away to change her nappy, and then immersed herself in taking care of laundry and house cleaning and shopping.

They ate sandwiches for lunch and Jess baked, and then put on a casserole so there'd be food for when Dan's children got back. Mid-afternoon she excused herself and went home.

Jess hadn't told Dan about her visits from Peter's parents but it could wait. There hadn't exactly been the right moment.

CHAPTER THIRTEEN

'Jess. It's . . . Dan.'

'Dan. What's the matter?' Jess had been sound asleep when her mobile phone started to ring. She'd leapt from bed and grabbed it, hoping the sound wouldn't wake Ella. It was still dark outside. The bedside clock said five a.m. Why would Dan call at this hour?

'I — don't feel right. One eye blurry. Face feels funny.' He drew a sharp breath. 'Called — to go to hospital.'

'Oh my God. Dan!' Jess snatched up the skirt she'd had on last night and pulled it on with the phone to her ear. 'You've called an ambulance?'

'Yes. Need you to come.'

A sick knot lodged itself deep inside Jess. 'I'm coming. I'll grab Ella and be right there, Dan.'

Jess disconnected and threw on the rest of her clothes, shoved her feet into sandals, snatched up Ella and the carry bag she always kept with her, and rushed to the car.

What was happening to Dan? He'd been struggling to speak. The symptoms sounded like a heart attack, didn't they, or a stroke? Either one was really bad!

She was at Dan's minutes later, in time to see Luke walk beside the officers as they loaded a gurney into the back of the ambulance. Dan was on that gurney. Jess drew up as close as she could, got Ella out and into her stroller in record time — her daughter was still more than halfway asleep — and hurried over. Her stomach lurched for Dan even as she worried how Luke would respond to her.

'Jess. I don't know what to do!' Luke blurted out the words without leaving his father's side. Tears formed in his eyes and he blinked them back fiercely.

'Stand back and let us load him, son.' The first ambulance officer caught Jess's gaze as he and the other man got Dan loaded into the back of the vehicle. 'Are you his partner?'

'Yes.' She was Dan's *working* partner and she loved him. That was enough as far as Jess was concerned. She wrapped her arm around Luke's shoulders and held on tight to the boy, and hoped he wouldn't get upset about that lie. 'Tell me what's wrong with him.'

'He'll be properly diagnosed at the hospital.'

'But you must have some idea.' Jess tried not to sound as worried as she felt. Beneath her hand, Luke's shoulders locked with tension.

'It's presenting as some form of stroke.'

'That's serious.' Luke made a choked sound, quickly stifled.

'We're going to take care of this, Luke. Your father's going to be all right.' Jess spoke almost sternly, but oh, she was terrified.

'Jess.' Dan said her name.

Jess's heart leapt into her throat as she curled her fingers around Dan's and held on. 'I'm here, Dan.' The words were choked. 'You need to get to the hospital.'

Worried eyes sought hers. 'Take care — ?'

'I will, Dan. I'll take care of everything.' Of course she would.

Jess turned to the nearest ambulance officer. 'Please!' She didn't know what she was begging for, only the taste of fear in her mouth. Nothing could happen to him!

Dan relaxed back onto the gurney. He caught his son's gaze with his eyes, and a moment later Luke had his arms around his father. Luke dry sobbed, once, and then the ambulance was on its way.

'We should have gone with him,' Luke said in a strangled tone as Jess hurried him inside. 'We could have woken everyone up.'

Jess struggled to think. 'I have to organise babysitting.' She needed to be at the hospital, to do whatever she could, ensure Dan got the best care. Anything! Jess snatched up the phone.

In what felt like an hour but was less than half that time, Jess had organised babysitting and was on the way to the hospital.

'Thanks — thanks for letting me come with you.' The words came uncertainly from Luke's mouth as Jess screeched her car to a halt in the closest visitor parking space at the hospital. She flung her door open and half jogged with Luke to the entrance.

'He's going to need you, Luke.' It was all she could manage for the worried boy. *Jess* was worried. Sick with it.

If anything bad happened to Dan . . . If she lost . . .

'You're scared, too.' Luke cleared his throat.

'Yes, Luke, I am.' Jess couldn't tell him she was even more scared because she'd fallen in love with his father. In Luke's mind that part of his father belonged to his mother and always would. Jess couldn't fight that out with Luke. Not now.

Maybe Luke, too, was too upset to think about it because he didn't say anything, just stuck to her side as she rushed to the front desk. 'Dan Frazier. He came in by ambulance.'

'Are you the partner?'

Jess glanced at Luke. 'Yes.'

'He's being cared for. You can take a seat for the moment.'

Jess and Luke sat. 'I wanted them to be open with me about his condition, Luke.'

'I know.'

It was a tense wait before they were allowed to slip in to see Dan briefly. He had a nurse watching him and he was in the intensive care unit.

There were monitors hooked up to him; his face was pale.

'Jess. Lukey.'

He couldn't be talking if he was really in trouble, could he?

'Dad.' Luke's breath rushed out of him. 'It took forever for them to let us in.'

There was so much else that Luke wasn't saying. Jess knew it because each and every fear was inside her, too. Was he all right? What had been happening while they were

200

closed out there? Was Dan going to be all right?

The nurse told them they couldn't stay long.

Jess went straight to the side of the bed and took Dan's hand. Luke hovered behind her until she reached with her other hand and drew him forward.

The affection in Dan's eyes made that action immediately worth it. 'Sorry. Worrying . . . everyone.'

'What happened, Dad?' Luke asked in a hushed tone.

'Wasn't too bad . . . Luke. Had . . .' He glanced at the nurse.

'Dan's had what we call a transient ischaemic attack.' The nurse held Jess's glance. 'This is sometimes referred to in lay terms as a mini stroke. Although it was quite scary, there aren't usually any lasting effects from this kind of attack. We just want to do our tests and make sure we take all the steps we can to ensure we don't have a bigger repeat.' She smiled at her patient. 'Don't we, Dan?'

'Yes.' A fierce expression came over his face. 'Going to get better.'

Luke swallowed and nodded. 'Of course you are, Dad.' His voice quavered before he added, 'You're not allowed to do anything else.' It was as close as the boy could come to asking Dan not to die.

Dan's glance moved between Jess and Luke. He looked worried.

Jess was worried.

Luke was worried.

And they had to pull together for Dan right now.

'Luke's been a great support, Dan.' Jess let her glance catch the boy's eyes before she looked back to Dan. 'And I organised babysitting before we got here.'

Jess had got one lady to look after Dan's children and Ella, and the other to care for her day-care children until further notice.

The nurse stepped forward. 'I'm going to have to ask you to leave now.' She looked at Jess. 'You can come back to check on him this evening. He needs to rest.'

'We have to go, Dan.' Jess didn't want to leave his side.

Dan nodded and caught his son's gaze again. 'Be fine, Luke.' His expression as he turned away showed he didn't believe this and Jess's heart lurched again.

Dan *had* to be fine!

The nurse ushered them out with kind efficiency whether they wanted to go or not.

When Jess got out into the reception area, she went straight to the desk. 'The nurse has explained a little of Dan's condition but I would really like to speak with the doctor as well, and if anything else happens I want to be notified immediately.'

'Of course.' The receptionist took details from Jess and gestured behind them. 'Take a seat. Doctor will be out to see you as soon as he can manage.'

They sat. They waited again. Should she send Luke away while she learned all of what had happened to Dan? 'It might be better if you leave me to speak with the doctor, Luke.'

'Please. Let me stay with you. If anything's — I'd rather . . .'

'All right, Luke.' One glance at his set face and Jess put the idea of shielding him out of her mind. She might not feel that Luke was old enough or mature enough to have to deal with something like this, particularly after losing his mother as he had, but it was happening anyway and keeping him in the dark about any of it wasn't going to help him.

Finally the doctor came out and addressed Jess. 'You're the partner?'

'Yes. Jessica Baker.' Jess gestured to Luke. 'This is Dan's eldest son.'

'Right. Well, the nurse has explained that

we believe Dan's had a transient ischaemic attack.'

'And that Dad won't have lasting symptoms from it,' Luke put in.

'That's usually correct though there can be permanent damage to the brain, but in the case of your father we're not concerned that there'll be anything nasty.' The man drew a breath before he went on. 'For now we've run some tests and will be conducting some further tests to determine what caused the TIA. He'll also be seen by a neurologist, and once we know where we're up to we'll be putting Dan on a plan to do everything we can to ensure that this remains an isolated, one-off incident.'

But that wasn't something that could be guaranteed? 'If it happened again — ?'

'It would most likely be a more serious event than this one.' The doctor went on to delve into various things that could cause a TIA. 'Dan's already let us know that he's probably getting too much salt in his diet, and not exercising enough. We'll see what else turns up as the result of our tests and what the neurologist thinks when he sees him.'

Until that moment, Jess hadn't fully let the seriousness of Dan's situation sink in. 'He's not old, he's healthy, even if he does eat too many packets of crisps and things.' The words blurted from her, but even as she said them her thoughts turned to what he'd been through in the past four years.

To him working so hard to get his family in a position where he could move them out of the city. Working mostly from home so he could care for the children full-time by himself, be fully responsible for them.

Had Dan even realised how much pressure he'd been putting on himself all the time? How much had he pushed down inside himself while he tried to be Superman to his family? Had that contributed?

'Why don't you go home, get some rest and give us a call this afternoon?' The doctor laid a hand briefly on Jess's arm. 'The best thing for our patient now is to rest, and I'm guessing that knowing things are under control at home will help with that. He was worried about you, and about his children.'

'I'll take care of everyone!' Tears tried to sting the backs of Jess's eyes at the thought of Dan worrying even for a minute about her in the middle of this.

She thanked the doctor and she and Luke made the trip back home.

'Jess — I'm . . . sorry for being . . . for not being nice to you.' Luke's low words stopped her before she could get out of the car when they arrived. 'It's just that Dad . . .'

'I know, Luke.'

'But you really care about him, don't you?' Luke swallowed hard. 'That way, I mean.'

'Yes.' Jess couldn't see the point of trying to hide something that Luke had recognised long ago. 'I do. But he doesn't —'

He didn't care about her in the same way. She couldn't choke the words out.

And she wasn't sure if Luke heard her, because the others had rushed outside all asking questions at once.

Jess helped Luke answer those questions, and counted the hours until she could go back to the hospital and see Dan again. She needed to see for herself that he truly was going to be okay.

The day dragged. Finally Jess was able to go back to the hospital. She took sleepwear for Dan, toiletries and anything else she felt he might use once he was allowed out of the intensive care unit.

The intimacy of packing for him didn't escape her, but now wasn't the time to dwell on those feelings. Jess needed to feel she was doing something for him.

'Is he truly doing okay?' Jess asked the duty nurse as she entered the intensive care unit. 'I phoned several times today and they said there hadn't been any more problems, but —'

'He's as well as we can hope.' This was a different nurse. She was brisk and not inclined to enter into any kind of dialogue. 'You can have five minutes with the patient and then you'll have to leave.' She turned her back to attend to one of the other patients.

Jess moved to Dan's bedside. His eyes were closed and his face looked drawn and pale. Her heart stumbled with fear and longing to tell him how much she loved him, to beg him to stick around, to not let anything happen that would take him from her, but she didn't have the right to those words with Dan. She didn't have the right to any of it.

'Jess. You're here.' Did his voice hold a hint of tenderness?

She searched his eyes. The face that she had come to know and love as she'd cared for his children.

That was what would be on Dan's mind. His babies, not his baby*sitter.*

'I'm here, Dan.' She clasped his hand because didn't they say that contact was healing? Jess pushed aside the thought that she was looking for healing for her own fears, too. 'The children are fine. They've been worried about you but I got a good sitter for as long as it's needed, and another one for my other day-care children. It's all taken care of.' Her voice turned husky as she pushed the rest of the words out. 'All you have to do is . . . get better.'

And not die on her. That was Jess's deepest fear. Luke's, too. The knowledge of that was what had pulled them together today, but it was a temporary fix. It didn't mean Luke would truly accept Jess, and Dan wasn't about to ask him to anyway.

'The doctors say I was lucky this time.' His fingers curled around hers. 'I'm worried about the children, Jess. Adele and Clive . . . love them, but they have their own lives. The kids already lost their mother. They need me.'

The raw honesty of Dan's words, of his fears for his family, wrapped around Jess's tender heart and squeezed. She forced her emotion back, couldn't let it out. Not now. She had to be strong for him. So that he could go on being strong for himself. 'You're going to recover, Dan. The doctors will tell you what you need to do to avoid —'

'A worse episode?' He swallowed. 'They've made it quite clear that's what I could expect if it happened a second time.'

She had known that, but it still struck fear

even deeper into her heart to hear him say it. 'Dan. Please . . . stay well, get better and . . . stay well.'

For his children. He probably thought she meant for the children and Jess did, but even deeper inside she meant for her. Would he please stay well for her?

Her fingers tightened around his hand, and his tightened too. Jess let herself lean forward then and wrapped her arms carefully around his shoulders. A sob tried to break free and she bit it back but for a moment she clung to him and every fear and uncertainty in her own life and now in his combined together into a deep well inside her. Dan's life was the only thing that would help her. Dan living, day in and day out, well and healthy and not under threat of being lost to her for ever.

Oh, Jess understood the fears of his children only too well, because they were deep inside her too.

The nurse bustled over to take Dan's readings, and told Jess she had to go. Jess got one last look at his face, murmured his name and the promise that she would be back in the morning.

'Have — have a good night, Dan. I'll see you in the morning.' She needed to hear the words, even if she spoke them aloud herself.

She *would* see Dan in the morning.

And Jess did, and visited him again that afternoon, and by the afternoon of the next day he'd been transferred to a normal ward and was able to have a visit from his children though they had to take turns going in two at a time.

Dan was starting to look better. But his concerns about the future remained in the backs of his eyes, and remained deep within Jess as well.

She heard from Dan's solicitor that she had no grounds to fight the situation with her cottage.

On the fifth day the doctor let Dan go home. Two days later Jess got a notice that her cottage would be auctioned one month from that day. She'd handed over care of her other day-charges to one of those two older women who'd helped out during Dan's hospitalisation.

At least she had a month to take care of Dan and to figure out what to do about accommodation for her and Ella. She'd heard from Ella's grandparents again, but hadn't been able to give them much more than a quick hello on the phone as she'd explained that her employer was sick in the hospital, though she did let them know that the auction date for the cottage had been set.

While Jess's heart ached constantly for Dan, for reassurance that he couldn't give her, to find some way to *make it* that he never got sick again, she focused on him and the children, and seeing to their needs. She slept at the house and expected everyone to understand, and they seemed to. Even Luke appeared grateful for her constant presence, and Jess was very careful, after her initial raw, unguarded fear for Dan, to try to be as professional as possible in front of all the children.

The next evening when the children were all in bed, Dan asked her to come out on the veranda with him. It reminded Jess of another night, of her first kiss with him on a swing seat. Jess had memories, too, of making love with Dan in his bed in his room here in the house. But she couldn't afford to torture herself with those memories.

She had a lot of needs when it came to him, but, for now, she could only do all she could to help with his recovery.

Dan watched expressions chase themselves across her face and gave thanks that he'd escaped this time with what was commonly called a mini stroke. The functional difficulties it had caused were gone. He was on doctor's orders about reducing salt in his diet, going for a walk every day, and there was a medication he had to take for a while until they felt it was safe for him to stop using it.

'I got off lightly this time.' He'd ended up facing his mortality anyway, and he needed to talk to Jess about it. Dan had done nothing but think of what could have happened if it had been worse. What if it had maimed him for life? Made it impossible for him to work? Or killed him? That was the one that worried Dan the most.

'You did get off lightly, Dan.' She drew a shaky breath.

As he searched her face beneath the veranda light where they stood side by side at the railing, Dan saw the stress and strain that Jess had been through since he called her on the phone that morning stamped across her face. 'I'm sorry it was hard on you, too, and I appreciate everything you did to look after the family.'

'Adele and Clive would have been here in a minute if you'd let them.' Jess turned to search his face. 'Your sister loves you and the children very much.'

'I know it.' He blew out a breath. 'She's in the early stages of pregnancy. They weren't planning to have any children, and she's a little older than is probably optimal. She's going to need to look after herself and —'

'Avoid stress? That's what I want you to do, too, Dan.' But she nodded to show she agreed with him.

'Jess, I'm going to do everything I can to try to make sure this isn't repeated, but I can't guarantee it.'

'I don't want that to happen to you again.' Her distress was real, and deep.

Dan's heart clenched. 'If something happens to me —'

'It won't! And I'll stay, Dan. I'll help for as long as you want.' Jess sucked up a breath. 'I don't need to find other work until . . . you don't need me any more.'

Her generosity humbled him. Her willingness to make her life work around his so she could help him . . . Well, Dan had a request that would be asking her to do even more of that. 'I want to ask you something, to put a suggestion to you that I hope might be of benefit to both of us in the end.'

Dan had thought and thought about it until he made the decision to ask her. He needed this reassurance if Jess could be prepared to give it. Needed it so he could know his children would be secure. That need had been all consuming for Dan since he suffered the TIA.

'What is it that you want to ask, Dan?' Jess frowned.

'I need to know my children will be in a secure situation if anything does happen to me.' When she would have protested again, he held up his hand. 'I'm not looking for that to happen. I want to live a long, healthy life and if I get to have any say in it that's exactly what's going to happen. But I can't control fate. This mini stroke made that abundantly clear to me. I want to get my children into the most secure position that I can, and I've come to realise that relying only on myself to care for them and be there for them has been rather arrogant of me. I've assumed things that I can't control.'

'Life is like that.' Jess's mouth tightened. 'There have been things in my life, too, that I haven't been able to control. They've just happened whether I felt ready for them or not.'

'Luke told me you got notice that your cottage is going to auction a month from now.' He said it gently because he knew that had to have cut Jess deeply.

Her shoulders tightened. 'I wasn't going to trouble you by telling you about that.'

'I wish you had.' He laid his hand over hers where it rested on the veranda railing. 'It's not fair for you to be dealing with the fallout of my visit to hospital, and trying to keep all your own worries away from me.'

And that brought Dan to the rest of what he wanted to say to her. Behind them he heard the faintest rustle of sound — a breeze picking up along the veranda?

Somehow it felt right to be holding Jess's hand as he said these words. Dan didn't love her but there were other things he could offer and maybe those would be enough?

'You need a home and security, Jess, and I need security for my children so I can stop worrying about them ending up without a parent.' His words were low, quiet, but spoken with conviction just the same. 'You and I — there's an attraction between us and I like to think there's at least some affection, too.'

Jess listened to Dan struggling through each word and her heart lodged very firmly in her throat because what was he saying? 'I don't understand, Dan.' She didn't. All she could comprehend was his hand over hers, how much she loved him, the need to keep him safe and the knowledge that Dan was right and she couldn't guarantee anything. Jess hated that fact.

'Will you marry me, Jess?' Dan's words were stronger as he asked the question, but then they quietened again. 'Help me to feel that I've made my children as secure as possible, and ensure security for you and Ella at the same time?' He turned her hand into his and searched her eyes, and his words became even quieter. 'I would do everything possible to be a good husband to you. I'd hope for a normal relationship between us. I realise there's not love, but —'

'What are you doing, Dad? You can't marry her! I don't want her in our lives like that. She's *not Mum!*' The words burst out from behind them.

Jess gasped and turned.

Dan turned, too.

But Luke had already disappeared back into the house with only the thunder of his feet as he ran up the stairs echoing behind him.

'I'll talk to him, Jess. The two of you were getting on so much better, I thought —'

That it had all been fixed? That Luke had calmed down and now wouldn't mind if Dan wanted to ask such a thing of Jess?

He was asking her to provide added security for his children, but to Luke that must sound as though Dan were trying to replace his mother. But Dan was very far from according Jess the place of a beloved wife in his heart.

'What you want is a practical arrangement.' Jess forced the words out. She made herself hold his gaze and not let him see for one moment how much his offer had built her hopes and devastated her, all at once. 'It's a big thing to ask and there *is* Luke to consider. He obviously feels passionately about this issue, maybe enough that you'll never get him to change his mind about me. I — I'll need time to think, and you will need to speak to him, Dan, and explain . . . that you don't . . . love me. That it's not about that.'

The words crushed her, but she forced them out anyway.

'I know you need time, Jess, and I will speak to Luke.' Dan drew a breath. 'It is a big issue for all concerned but it is an arrangement I believe could be helpful to all of us.'

It was bigger than Dan could know, because Jess loved him. All that he'd said was true, but there was one key thing that he didn't understand. While he would be trying to be a good husband and feeling affection for her, Jess would be madly and deeply in love with him.

That wasn't an even situation, and Jess didn't know if she could take it on. Security for her and Ella, yes, that was a factor that mattered to her and she appreciated Dan was trying to offer something that would benefit everyone. How could she say no when he needed this to feel safe, and to make sure his children were safe?

Jess loved all of them, prickly Luke included, though obviously she loved Dan very differently.

Heart, soul, mind, body and spirit.

The words pushed through her, came from deep inside her. And suddenly she couldn't stand here any longer, looking into his eyes and . . . loving him with everything she had. 'I — I need to go to bed, Dan. I'll think, and you might change your mind once you speak to Luke —'

'It won't happen, Jess.'

Because there was no comparison to Rebecca, and Dan would help his son understand that?

Jess whirled away before he could see the emotions on her face. She got to her bedroom, closed the door, and then and only then did she allow all of what she was feeling to come.

Jess was being offered what her heart most desired, a future with Dan, but without the love. With Ella's father, she might have made a huge mistake in trusting him, but at least in the beginning she had truly believed she loved him. That love hadn't been returned in the same measure, any more than Dan's would be.

Dan should be asking Jess to marry him because he loved her. She had a right to expect that. But it was still true that it would solve problems for both of them.

And just to confuse things for her further, Jess now had Ella's grandparents, who wanted to be part of her daughter's life.

Which was truly wonderful.

It was, but where did this all leave Jess?

CHAPTER FOURTEEN

'And so you see, dear, Lang Fielder was planning the whole time to get your property off you cheaply. He intended to knock it down along with the three others he already owns in this area and have enough money to pay for the mansion he wants to build on the site.' George Rosche was again seated in Jess's kitchen in the cottage. 'All it took was for him to move into that position at the council and get control of the situation with the notices about the back rates on your home.'

Dalia sat beside George.

Ella was tottering about the kitchen showing off her new walking skills to both grandparents.

And Jess was sitting like a stunned fish, trying to comprehend what had just been said to her.

George and Dalia had phoned and asked her to see them urgently. Dan was well

220

enough for Jess to decide to meet them here at her cottage. Maybe while she was absent Dan would take the chance to speak to Luke about asking Jess to marry him.

'Jess, the man had no right to let that situation go for the length of time that he did and not inform you of what was happening. He had his own agenda from the start.' Dalia's fury on Jess's behalf warmed her heart.

Dalia glanced at her husband and said in a rush, 'Well, it made us cross and I do hope you understand, dear. We're Ella's grandparents and it's clear to us that you're a very special girl. You shouldn't have been treated the way you were by our son.'

'Just tell her,' George put in.

Dalia drew a breath. 'We paid off the back rates and interest so that nasty man couldn't go ahead with his plans. The auction is cancelled. The cottage is yours now fair and square.'

'We could easily afford it, so don't worry about that.' George nodded. 'But you should still bring this man's actions to the attention of council's management. He should be sacked for such underhanded dealings. We'll be more than happy to help you with that, if you want.' He made a hurrumph of sound. 'It will serve the man right, too.'

'The times that I went to the council and

had to practically beg to see him, and he encouraged me to pay what I could off the debt knowing that he planned to buy the cottage out from under me for practically nothing.' Jess spoke the words in shock and anger. 'I will speak to management at the council.'

She searched both their faces before she added almost uncertainly, 'If you really wouldn't mind, the added support while I do that —'

'We would like to help you.' George said it quietly but his expression was completely sincere.

Jess almost didn't know how to respond to their supportiveness. She was used to standing alone, to having no choice but to make her own way, her own decisions. What would it be like if she married Dan? Would he be planning for them to support one another in that way? Could Jess live with that, a gift of support but no love?

She needed to figure out the answer.

But first she had to deal with this. And as that thought came Jess fully comprehended what the couple had done. 'George, Dalia, thank you for what you've done for me.' They'd been so generous! 'I — I'll need to pay that money back to you. It's yours and in the end you don't owe me anything.'

'We know that's how you feel about us, dear.' Dalia leaned forward to pat Jess's hand where it rested on the table. 'But you were struggling, and that situation wasn't right. It wasn't a difficult thing for us. Please, just accept it? There are no strings attached of any kind. We don't want you to feel pressured, even to let us be part of Ella's and your life, though we would really love that. Peter is our only child and, well, we never thought there'd be a grandchild or a lovely young woman who is her mother.'

They talked for a while longer. And Jess did accept the gift, but more importantly made it very clear that she welcomed their involvement in Ella's life and always would. She swallowed. 'Family isn't something that I've had much of for myself and if Ella can have that with you, and a little for me too, well, I want it.'

With that decided, George asked if it might not be best to go to the council now and confront the issue of Lang Fielder's behaviour.

Jess drew a deep breath and nodded. This had to be done and the sooner the better. They took separate cars and made their way there. When the clerk tried to refuse to allow them to see the manager, Jess threw her shoulders back. 'We're not leaving until this is done.'

They were ushered into the manager's office. Jess drew a deep breath and explained the situation. The manager was clearly shocked and blustered somewhat. Jess stuck her chin out. 'I want you to call Lang Fielder in here. Ask him what he was planning to do and how he intended to go about it.'

The manager took the time to access council records before he called the other man in. Once he did, he spread out the evidence before him and looked at Lang. 'I thought I knew you, Fielder, but clearly I didn't. If this is the kind of illegal activity you can carry on in your place of work, I want no part of you. Your position here is terminated, effective immediately.'

'You can't do that. I'll file a complaint —'

'And while you're doing that, I'll be investigating every other matter that you've handled since you started work here.' The manager stared Lang down. 'You should hope there won't be formal charges either from the council or from Miss Baker.'

Lang glared back, and after a long moment he stalked to the office door and yanked it open. 'You haven't heard the end of this.'

It was an empty threat and the manager

said as much once he closed the door behind Lang and phoned through to staff to let them know the situation so they could see Lang safely off the premises.

The manager shook his head, apologised again to Jess, and after some further discussion in which he assured her the issue would be fully dealt with they were ushered out.

'Thank you.' As they stood outside Jess impulsively hugged the older couple.

George and Dalia said their goodbyes and left. Jess put Ella into the car and drove to Dan's.

She now truly owned her cottage and it couldn't be taken from her. There was security in that, and kindness from Ella's grandparents. More than that, they wanted to be part of Ella's life and they wanted to be part of *Jess's* life, too.

'Family, Ella,' Jess murmured quietly. 'We've been given some family who — really want us.'

The last words were a little choked, and Jess quickly cleared her throat. Dan had also asked her to be part of his family. She needed to give him her answer. Why couldn't she just go to him and say yes? Wasn't that in everyone's best interests?

The situation has changed now that you own the cottage outright.

But Dan's need to make his children secure hadn't changed, and his wish to make Jess his wife hadn't changed. She would have the chance to love him, even if he didn't love her back . . .

'Time to go inside, Ella. We at least need to find out whether Dan's spoken with Luke, and how that went.'

'Jess. I hope you had enough time with Ella's grandparents.' Dan searched Jess's face.

He wasn't sure what had happened but whatever it was, he would try to help. He was waiting for her answer to his proposal. He hadn't found that waiting period easy but he respected her need to think. He hadn't even known that Ella's grandparents wanted to start a relationship so they could get to know their grandchild until Jess asked him for some time off this morning.

'Dan, did you speak with Luke?'

There was something in Jess's tone that made him immediately tense.

'I did.' Dan had spoken to his son, explained that he wasn't trying to replace Rebecca in any of their lives.

Luke had cried a little. Dan wished he'd realised what was buried within his son. 'I didn't know he'd held on to a lot of the pain from the loss of his mother. He . . . let some of it out with me, and I think over time he'll continue that process.'

'That's good, Dan.' Jess was happy to know that he had got to the bottom of Luke's pain and that his son looked as though he could start to go forward now.

'He won't stand in the way, Jess, if we . . .'

If they married. If they tried to become firm friends who would help one another through life and with the various children.

Jess nodded.

'I need to tell you about Ella's grand-parents.' She sought for the right words and in the end just told him, as concisely as she could, what had happened about the cot-tage and Lang Fielder's dismissal from the council. 'I own my cottage now, fair and square. George and Dalia have been very generous. Most of all, even more than the money, I value that they cared enough to help me, and to help me get justice for the way Lang Fielder tricked me and tried to cheat me.'

Dan listened to Jess's words. There was hurt hiding underneath her anger over Councillor Fielder's behaviour. He could see that and as he looked into her eyes and felt all her pain as though it were his own Dan realised there were things he'd been holding back from letting himself acknowledge. He'd spoken to Luke and said all the words that he'd felt were the right ones, but even then he hadn't realised . . .

'My money worries are over, Dan.' Jess said it as though the fact was only beginning to sink in for her. At her feet, Ella started to grizzle, and Jess picked her up and cuddled her and the little girl tucked her head into her mother's neck.

Jess went on. 'The cottage is secure thanks to Ella's grandparents, the parents of Peter Rosche. Too bad if Peter made me sign something saying I'd never tell his name. He broke his end of the bargain and his parents came and found me and asked to be part of Ella's life and wanted me as well anyway!'

'That's really special news, Jess.' He meant that.

'I would never have let George and Dalia pay off the money owed to the council if I'd known what they planned to do.' She chewed her lip.

Ella decided she'd had enough cuddles and wriggled. Jess set her down and she went straight to play with a set of large blocks on the floor.

'But they did it anyway.' They probably felt guilty for the way their son had treated her. Not their fault, but Dan would have been the same. 'It sounds as though they really needed to do that for you, Jess, as much as it was a help to you.'

And he couldn't help asking himself how this would impact on her answer to him.

She didn't need him now. Not the way she had before Ella's grandparents came along.

But he . . . needed her.

His heart squeezed. For a moment he felt panicked, wondered if he was about to repeat the mini stroke.

But it hadn't felt like this.

And as he took a breath he realised *why* his heart had just felt as though someone had locked a fist around it. He didn't want to lose Jess. He wanted her to agree to be his wife. For his children, for security. But most of all Dan wanted that for himself. It was the one part of it that he had failed to see.

He'd . . . fallen in love with Jess.

Dan hadn't believed he could ever do that again. He'd thought all of his love had been for Rebecca. He had fallen for Jess differently, but just as deeply as he'd loved his wife. No wonder he hadn't known exactly how to explain things to Luke. Dan hadn't understood his own feelings.

'Dan, I have to give you my answer. I

don't want you to have to wait any longer.'

At her words, he sought her gaze and realised he could have made a complete mess of all of this. He'd asked her to marry him for worthy reasons, but those reasons hadn't allowed for how Jess might feel emotionally about him, for the fact that he loved her and needed to know if she could love him in return.

Could he convince Jess to love him in the way that he loved her? Could he help her to trust him, even though Peter Rosche had hurt her? Even though Dan was older? And though he'd been so slow to recognise his feelings prior to making that proposal? Could Dan help his children to accept that he loved Jess and needed her to be in his life?

Dan needed to speak to his children and he needed to do his proposal to Jess over, and this time do it properly. He realised that, as well as Luke needing to adjust, and maybe the others too, though he knew they all had a lot of affection for Jess already, *he* had to fully let go of Rebecca. He should have done it a long time ago. He needed to take this final step.

'Jess, would you let me speak to you about that tonight? After the children have gone to bed?' He wanted to take the time to give her something special for when he asked those words a second time.

Rob and Daisy started squabbling outside on the veranda and Jess got up to go and investigate. 'I guess that would be a better time.'

As she went about her work in the home Dan went into his den and picked up the phone so he could start making his plans for the night.

'You and the children were quiet when you got back after your walk.' Jess tried to keep the nervous edge out of her tone.

Dan had taken the children for a walk on the property a few hours ago. He'd had something in a carry bag with him, and a shovel. They'd been gone quite a while. When they got back, they had all seemed subdued, surprised, emotional somehow . . .

And then Mary had hesitated, run forward and hugged Jess around the knees and skittered off again. Daisy had tipped her head on the side and looked at Jess and then at Ella and she'd seemed somehow to make a decision. She'd given a nod of her head and taken Annapolly by the hand and they'd gone inside.

Rob had looked at Jess, too, and then looked away as though embarrassed and she thought he might have had evidence of earlier tears on his face.

And Luke . . .

One glance at Luke's face had told her the boy had been through something deeply emotional. If Dan had spoken to them all about marrying her and this was the re-action —

But then Luke had wrapped his arms around his father's middle and hugged him hard and let out a deep sigh as though a weight had lifted from his shoulders and then he, too, had gone inside.

Now it was just Jess and Dan and it was evening. Ella was sleeping in the travel cot. Dan had asked Jess to go home and change into something pretty and meet him back here. He was getting the other caregiver in to stay with the children, and he and Jess were going . . . out, but some place quite close.

Jess was mystified, a little uneasy, trying not to wonder just what Dan was up to and why she would need to wear a nice dress to discuss the future. Dan had already made what he wanted from her quite clear. Did he need to call it all off because his children hadn't been able to accept the idea?

But she dressed in her pretty dress, and Dan — Dan wore black dress trousers and shoes and a crisp pale green shirt.

Jess glanced at her yellow sundress with the big red and orange flowers splashed all over it. 'I hope I'm dressed appropriately for the occasion.' The dress had a square neckline and flared about her knees. She'd teamed it with her row of wooden bangles and the chunky wooden necklace and just a little understated make-up.

'You look perfect for where we're going.' Dan crooked his elbow and gave a half smile.

If Jess hadn't known him so well she might have missed the edge of tension beneath that smile. But she did know him, and she did see it. She linked her hand through his arm and he . . . led her to the tree cubby house!

'Shall we, Jess? It seems to be the right place for this discussion.'

Somehow they were at the top of the ladder and inside the space, and oh —

'It's beautiful.' The whole place was decorated with bouquets of flowers — store-bought ones that must have cost him a fortune! There was a picnic blanket on the floor again, scatter cushions to lean on. A bucket with . . . wine in it? Two beautiful fluted glasses and a platter of colourful fruit pieces.

Her heart started to pump hard. What was he doing?

Dan took her hand and led her to the picnic blanket. 'Shall we sit, Jess?'

His hand shook slightly as he poured the wine and handed her one of the flutes.

'You didn't have to do this.' She chose a grape from the platter and popped it into her mouth. The sweet taste blended with the taste of wine on her tongue. 'I know that what you offered, well, that it isn't all about romance really or . . . feelings, and I'd already made up my mind to tell you . . . but of course if the children —'

'I'm hoping that I might be able to start all that over, Jess.' He set down his wine-glass. He'd barely taken a sip.

All she knew was that she loved him and she was prepared to take the risk of marrying him and hope that his affection for her would be enough. She couldn't think of living life without seeing him. If this gave her the opportunity to be with him then Jess wanted to take that chance. And it *seemed* as though he wasn't trying to tell her that he'd changed his mind after speaking with his children. 'You're not withdrawing — ?'

If he did she would find a way to handle it. She would. Jess didn't know how, but she was strong. She'd do it if she had to.

'I asked you to marry me primarily to give security to my children, and to you.' He took her hand in his again and his fingers gently stroked over hers.

'I know, and even without me needing that help any more, what you asked for the children was very valid.' Jess drew a breath. 'I care about them, Dan. They've all found their way into my heart.'

Being with Dan would give Jess and Ella a sense of family, too, something Jess had never expected to have. She'd gained grand-parents for Ella, and all this. She was determined to appreciate it. 'Ella will have siblings to love and grow up with. I really value that.'

'And I value you, Jess.' He drew a breath. 'You're generous and giving and kind. I love your beautiful clothes and accessories that are so much a part of who you are. I love that you're so determined about life and how cheerful you are even when things are tough.'

'I'm not always cheerful.' She had her moments, and she remembered one such, just after she'd found out about the auction on the cottage. 'Well, you've seen that.'

'I've seen a lot of different parts of you, Jess.' His fingers curled around hers and his voice deepened. 'I took the children today and we went to that big old tree down at the end of the property.'

'So you could talk to them about the possibility of marrying me?'

'Yes. And we took Rebecca's ashes and buried them beneath the tree.'

'Oh, Dan.' Emotion clogged her throat. 'That can't have been easy.'

'It was something that we all needed, I think.' He smiled and there was only peace on his face as he went on. 'I hadn't totally let go, Jess. I'd been holding on to how much I'd loved Rebecca so that I wouldn't have to face the risk of fully living my life again. I told myself, because the children had grieved and I'd helped them and time had passed, that I'd done all I had to as well, but that wasn't true.'

'You've done a wonderful job with the children, Dan.' Her fingers squeezed right back around his. 'And you're not to blame for loving your wife so much that you knew you could never love again like that. I understand.'

Dan drew closer to her until they were both leaning back on the cushions and his shoulder was brushing hers. Their hands were still intertwined. 'I thought that was what I knew, but, Jess . . . I did fall in love again. I fell deeply, but I hadn't realised what was happening until I made a proposal for good reasons, but not for the *right* reasons, and Luke carried on about it and you said you'd work out your answer.

'When you came in this morning and told me that Ella's paternal grandparents had paid off the money owed on your cottage, I knew you didn't *need* me for security.' His mouth softened. 'It was then that I realised *I needed you* for myself, because I was in love with you. I hoped that I hadn't messed everything up by asking you to marry me for those other reasons.'

'Oh, Dan.' Could she believe what she was hearing? Her heart had hoped so desperately for Dan to love her but she hadn't expected it. 'But there *is* Luke. I don't want to hurt him, Dan.'

'And I . . . love you for that.' Dan drew a breath. 'Luke saw feelings in me towards you that I hadn't recognised myself for what they were. Today I admitted everything to him and we talked openly about the loss of his mother, all of it. I think Luke will really be able to fully heal now, and he does understand that I care for you because you're you. It's no reflection on that past relationship.'

Dan's gaze held hers and his expression became very serious. 'I learned that I can love deeply, twice over, Jess. I was worried for the security of my children. That stopped me from recognising and accepting what I was feeling towards you. I can't guarantee anything in life, but I want the chance to love you with all my heart. I hope for you and I to have very long lives together.'

'I was going to say yes, Dan.' She admitted it as love spread through her heart, too, set free finally by his words. 'I fell in love with you the night that we made love. I *realised it* the next morning when Ella walked to you. When you asked me to marry you I wasn't sure what I should say. I wanted to be with you, but I was afraid that it might hurt too much to love you and not be loved in the same way in return. I . . . went through that with Peter.'

'You would have said yes for the children's sakes.'

'For all of us, really, but only if you'd been able to assure me you felt confident we could get Luke into a better frame of mind about it all.' Jess could understand why people would make choices to keep their children safe. 'I love that about you, Dan. I've admired your commitment to your family from the first day we met.'

'I fell in love with all of you.' He ran his fingers over the bangles on her arm until

238

they clanked together. 'The way you came to me and offered help even in the face of your own problems. Your care of the children. Your love for your daughter.'

'I'm hopeful that I can build a good relationship with Ella's grandparents.'

'I think you're already well on the way to that, and, if you give me the chance, I'll support it every step of the way.' Dan blew out a breath and then searched her face. 'Will you marry me, Jess? Because I love you and need you in my life?'

'I love you and need you too. You have my whole heart.' Oh, how good it felt to say those words. She was finally able to open all of her heart and give it to this man, and know that it would be safe with him. 'Yes, I will marry you. I will love you, and love your children, and spend the rest of my life enjoying every aspect of all of you.'

'Thank you.' He kissed her then, a deep, reverent kiss that held all of his love, and allowed Jess to give all of her love back to him.

When they finally drew apart, Dan's expression sobered. 'I can't guarantee — with what happened with that mini stroke —'

'I know.' Jess understood the concerns only too well. She would carry them buried in the back of her heart probably for a long time. 'You're doing all the right things to look after yourself and put yourself in the best place to avoid a repeat of that.'

It was all Jess could ask. All that Dan could ask of life, as well. 'You're right, Dan. There are things that happen that we can't control. I will hope and pray for your health and the chance to love you long into the future.' And then she smiled. 'And I'll control your salt intake whether you like it or not. No more stashes of salty snacks for you.'

'I know. I'll behave.' His laugh was rich and full of promise. He wrapped his arms around her while he was still chuckling. She felt the vibrations of his humour as he held her, and she smiled too.

'I'd like to stay out here and make love to you, Jess.' He said it with longing in his tone, but also with a degree of resignation.

'But there are a bunch of children and a fill-in caregiver waiting inside for the out-come of this meeting?'

'Yes. I suspect that's how it's going to be.'

She got to her feet and held out her hand to him. 'It won't always be easy or smooth sailing, but I am excited about the future. Let's go inside and tell them the news.'

It hit her then, really, that she was about

to become stepmother to five children and a hint of panic surfaced. 'Will they be okay with this? In the end, at least?'

He got to his feet and brought her hand to his lips. 'Like me, they know they are getting the joy and pleasure of being able to love a second time. I think even Luke will come to appreciate that deeply in the end.'

His words brought moisture to her eyes, but she blinked and let her joy come through. 'This is the start of the rest of all our lives together.'

'Marry me soon, Jessica.' Dan's voice softened with love and need. 'A wedding right here beside the house, with all the children as attendants. We'll make a beautiful setting for it. Ella and Daisy and Mary and Annapolly can wear pretty dresses and garlands of silk flowers. We'll make Rob and Luke dress in tuxedos. I want to see you in a beautiful bridal gown as I exchange rings with you.'

'Then we'll do all of that, Dan.' She whispered the words. 'I will marry you very soon right here.'

He swept her into his arms and kissed her again, and then led her out of the tree house and back inside so they could share their good news . . .

ABOUT THE AUTHOR

Australian author **Jennie Adams** grew up in a rambling farmhouse surrounded by books and by people who loved reading them. She decided at a young age to be a writer, but it took many years and a lot of scenic detours before she sat down to pen her first romance novel. Jennie has worked in a number of careers and voluntary positions, including transcription typist and preschool assistant. She is the proud mother of three fabulous adult children and makes her home in a small inland city in New South Wales. In her leisure time, Jennie loves taking long, rambling walks, discovering new music, starting knitting projects that she rarely finishes, chatting with friends, going to the movies and new dining experiences.

Jennie loves to hear from her readers, and can be contacted via her website at www .jennieadams.net.